Ivan Arthur is the author of five books, *Pavement Prayers*, *Brands under Fire*, *Once More upon a Time*, *Jossie* and *The Fourteen Stations*, and confesses to two hibernating blogs, 'Excalibur' and 'Thurifer'. Arthur is a three-time winner of the WPP international Atticus Award for original writing. An advertising professional, Ivan Arthur was the former Area Creative Director of JWT, in charge of India, Sri Lanka, Pakistan and Bangladesh and went on to be inducted into India's Communication Arts Guild Hall of Fame. As Vice-Chairman and trustee, he designed and conducted the Communication Specialization at the Asian Institute of Communication and Research. He lives with his wife in Goa.

A
Village
Dies

Your invitation to a memorable funeral

IVAN ARTHUR

SPEAKING
TIGER

SPEAKING TIGER PUBLISHING PVT. LTD
4381/4 Ansari Road, Daryaganj,
New Delhi–110002, India

Copyright © Ivan Arthur 2016

ISBN: 978-93-86050-14-4
eISBN: 978-93-86050-73-1

10 9 8 7 6 5 4 3 2 1

Typeset in Adobe Garamond Pro by SÜRYA, New Delhi
Printed at Gopsons Papers Ltd., Noida

They pop up
between the truth and the lies in my tale,
pointing fingers of reprove and glee
at things that might not
or might have happened.
I present to the eternal diaspora
of Amboli and Kevni under the tombstones,
my mischievous fantasies as tribute.

Contents

Author's Note

THIS IS A WORK OF FICTION SET IN THE VILLAGE I GREW UP in. While the main story is fictional, it is built around the jagged corners of a few real events, some of which may be vivid in the minds of some from my generation or even those much younger; some of them are just moments from the misty memories of my childhood. The Raman Raghavan episode is one that became known not just in Mumbai but globally, while incidents such as the burning of the mutton shop or the mini-war between Amboli and Kevni would be remembered, if at all, by a few old-timers of the two villages. The main characters are figments of my imagination, but I have garnished the narrative with a few real people (I have used their real names) who, in my mind, embodied the very soul of the twin villages and whose personalities, I believe, were almost linked to the geography of the place.

Amboli and Kevni of the 1940s were a cluster of homes owned almost entirely by East Indians, the original inhabitants of the place. The East Indians were one of the three communities of Portuguese Christians, the other two being the Goans and the Mangaloreans. They called themselves East Indians (placing diplomacy and strategy over geographic correctness) for an opportunistic alignment with the powerful East India Company, thus separating themselves from the Goans and the Mangaloreans. This would give them an edge over the other two groups in the job market of those days. For this reason, they even slipped out of their quaint East Indian Marathi dialect into the English language which, like an ill-fitting garment, had to be altered to fit the local tongue.

Which brings us to the use of language in this narrative.

The three communities communicated with each other in an English of sorts, an English spliced with the vocabulary, grammar, accents and phonetics of their native tongues. The Goans and Mangaloreans spoke their respective forms of Konkani at home; out of home, in the markets and grocery stores, they spoke Marathi and Hindi. With the other Catholics in the parish, they spoke—well, let's call it—'English'. The East Indians, both at home and outside, spoke a fusion of 'English' and the East Indian Marathi dialect. Minglish? Maringlish? A forerunner, if you will, of the 'Hinglish' made popular by latter-day advertising (*Yeh hi hai right choice, baby*). H's were dispensed with: so 'thing' was rendered as 'ting', 'mother' as 'mudder', even among the more lettered among them. The result was a new dialect of the English language, exclusively owned by the East Indians of Amboli, Kevni and other East Indian villages of the suburbs, a micro-dictionary of words and phrases that Fowler might have gleefully put down in a page or two.

In my earlier book, *Jossie*, I had ventured to do just that—to put together a useable Lexicon of Ambolingish. Here it is for what it is worth.

The Amboli lexicon, you will see, was not unnecessarily profligate with vocabulary. It would make do with a few words—while the world used a hundred—to communicate the stuff of everyday living. Amboli used a single word to deliver a whole thesaurus of meaning, the ultimate sense being conveyed more by context than vocabulary. It was a semantic ingenuity that could only be designed by Amboli.

From the Amboli Lexicon/Thesaurus:

Hopeless: |ˈhōplis| Adjective

　　Bad: *Hopeless buggar*, no good, horrible, wicked, avoidable, dangerous, unfriendly, hateful, anathema on him

　　Snooty: *She hopeless ting*, proud, uncooperative, ugly, plain, ordinary, unsociable, masculine, rough

　　Strict: *He hopeless padre*, severe, boring, loud, punishing, self-righteous, unholy, probably promiscuous, corrupt, avoidable confessor

Spoilt: *This is hopeless fish, menn*, stale, stinking, tasteless, too expensive, unaffordable

Difficult: *Today exam was hopeless, no?* Stiff, unfair, disappointing, depressing, forgettable

Tuneless: *What hopeless numbers she sang*, old-fashioned, irrelevant, unfamiliar, classical, not popular

Nice: |nīs| adjective:

Decent: *He's a nice buggar*, good, gentle, bit of a sucker, naïve, easy-going, friendly, safe, okay, passable, approved

Ladylike: *Nice ting, Aunty Philoo*, demure, kind, sweet, generous, amenable, effete

Hard: *He gave him nice pasting*, vigorous, thorough, sound, earnest, forceful, powerful, heavy, hurtful

Tasty: *Nice cake became*, delicious, sweet, palatable

Big: *Nice house, menn*, large, robust, tough, durable, good-looking, strong, worth buying, enviable

Sexy: *Nice bum, menn*, sensuous, sensual, sinful, tempting, alluring, wicked

Buggar: |ˈbəgər|. Noun.

Man: *I saw the buggar standing there*, guy, chap, fellow

Bugger: *Lazy buggar*, a no-good, etc

Friend: *Come on you buggar, let's have uttara, menn*, partner, comrade, drinking buddy

Villain: *He's a dutty buggar*, bad man, untrustworthy,

dangerous, avoidable, cheat, not our type, unfriendly, sophisticated

Ting: noun
Girl: *She's a nice ting, no?* Lady, woman, lass, maid, damsel (Amboli's traditional morality stripping the distaff side of all sexuality, gender-based vocabulary evoking possible sensuous visions)

Became: |bə'kem|verb (generally in the past tense)
Born: *Six months marry and baby became, how no?*
Made: *Chappatti became what?* Done, completed, finished, accomplished
Took place: *Gundowli buggars came here and fight became,* happened, caused
Resulted in: *You did not listen and see what haal became!*

Menn: |men| Verbal punctuation (full stop, comma, exclamation with contextual meaning: man, fellow, you bum, my beloved, idiot, my friend …)

Some of the characters in this book speak Ambolinglish, which, I assure you, will not be difficult to understand within its context. Hindi, Marathi and Konkani words have been instantly translated wherever they did not weigh the sentence down.

I have also included a glossary/translation of words and phrases at the end of the book.

Hanging Gardens

Hanging Gardens lay there in his coffin, hands tied together stiffly over his chest, fingers reluctantly entwined in frozen prayer. It was a cheap coffin draped in the customary virginal white of the unmarried deceased.

Kitty did a fifty-year subtraction over his face. That was about how long ago she had first seen him. He hadn't changed much since then, she thought. The round, dark face with its big, flared nostrils and thick lips was remarkably unchanged, with hardly any wrinkles. Those bushy eyebrows had a few overgrown strands of grey. Some grey too in his thick mop of hair, but not much. It was as if Hanging Gardens had died fifty years ago and was being buried today. Time had passed kindly over his countenance. That, Kitty thought, was the consolation prize of simpletons and virgins.

She remembered that day half a century ago. She was going home from school. Class II. Miss Aida's class. 'Aida-Baida,' the other classes teased (baida being the Mumbai slang for egg) and Kitty would lash out at them with her small six-year-old hands, defending her teacher's name. Oh, she was quite a little thing then. Stood her ground against even the bullies of the higher classes. She loved playing games, all games. Even boys' games: marbles, tops, gully cricket and kite-flying. So the bigger boys teased as they ran past her: 'Kitty, Kitty tomboy; half-girl and half-boy.' Bringing those little six-year-old hands out for action.

Her classroom was in the corridor leading from the church sacristy to the assistant parish priest's room. That day, school bag over her shoulder (backpacks were not known then, in the late 1940s), she exited the compound from the small rear gate. It led to a narrow lane which wound all the way down a ten-minute walk to her home. Left of the lane was the two-storeyed house in which Miss Aida lived with her brother's family. On the right was another small lane where Aunty Mae and her husband had their one-storeyed house. (Aunty Mae was Aunty Mae to everyone, from toddlers to old men.)

Usually as she stepped out of the gate onto the tarred road, she would hurry home, as instructed by her parents, without stopping to speak to strangers. There were rumours that 'the catching lorry' was out, looking for little children who, it was said, would be taken and sacrificed to Kali for the successful construction of some bridge or public building. Kali would be appeased only by the blood of little children, they said. 'Rubbish!' her father dismissed these whispers as nonsense. 'Kitty has to hurry home because she has to hurry home. Nothing more than that.'

But on that day, she stopped in her tracks. In front of her was something she did not like at all. She saw two of her neighbours, Cliffy and Dominic, both twice her age, giving Hanging Gardens a hard time. Hanging Gardens was not his real name. It was given to him by the boys of Kevni village because of his untreated hernia and hydrocele, visible as a big swinging bulge through his pants. Hanging Gardens wore what was given to him by the St. Vincent de Paul Society: shirts, shorts and trousers that did not always fit. He secured his pants with a cord tied round his waist. Most often, he could be seen holding his pants up to keep them from falling. And Hanging Gardens never wore underwear; probably didn't know what they were. So the bulge kept dangling, like a sack of onions between his legs as he walked. He hardly ever spoke and when he did, it was in incoherent, salivary monosyllables that an attentive ear might discern as Konkani, Hindi, Marathi or rather a simultaneous polyglotism.

Hanging Gardens was a good six or seven years older than Cliffy and Dominic. He was also much bigger made. He had bulging muscles from all the hard work that he had to do as the village handyman. One swing of his big palm would be enough to send both Cliffy and Dominic flying. But then, Hanging Gardens was a docile giant, slow in gait, speech and understanding. He would not lift a finger to hurt even an angry dog. The boys of the village ran after him, teasing and making fun of him. 'Hanging Gardens!' they sang as he passed by. He just kept walking, seemingly deaf to it all, responding with neither smile nor scowl.

Kitty saw that Cliffy and Dominic had him trapped between them. Both had sticks in their hands. 'Hanging Gardens, Hanging Gardens,' they sniggered. From behind, Cliffy had succeeded in pulling the fellow's pants down with his stick. Kitty saw between the poor man's legs what looked like those brown-stained muslin rags used by chai shops to strain tea; only this was many times bigger. From the opposite side, Dominic prodded the descended and enlarged scrotum with his stick. Hanging Gardens roared in pain. He held on to his scrotum and wept loudly, jumping up and down, yelping piteously like a wounded animal, each jump causing much glee to his two tormentors, who continued prodding that painful pouch between his legs.

Kitty put her school bag down, picked up a stone big enough to fit into her small palm and flung it with all her strength. It caught Dominic on his temple. He fell, clutching his head. In the pause that ensued, Kitty saw an angry Cliffy come threateningly towards her with a stick. She did not budge. Unblinking, she bent down again, picked up another small rock and waited. Cliffy stopped, deciding what to do next. By then, a small crowd of children had collected to watch 'the fun'. At that moment

Cliffy felt his collar being grabbed from behind him. It was his father, who looked at him with fury. 'Come home,' he said, 'I'll show you hanging gardens.' Then, looking sternly at Dominic, he said, 'That was not nice, baba. Wait till your father hears of this.' Holding Kitty's hand, he walked her home, with Cliffy walking in front of them.

Kitty's home was two chawls away from Henry Chawl where Cliffy lived, but even from her house, she could hear him bawling as his father's belt came down heavily on the boy's back.

Caesar Road

HALF A CENTURY SEEMED LITTLE MORE THAN A FEW TORN calendar sheets gone; and now, looking at that face, not yet coffin-covered for eternity, Kitty felt that Change was no more than a thin translucence over the remembered past. Not much had changed. Now a visitor in her own parish (Muscat, and then Dubai, being the home she couldn't quite call home for the past two decades), Kitty looked for changes every time her taxi brought her from Santa Cruz airport to Amboli naka. She looked up from Hanging Gardens' face and turned her gaze towards the church, St. Blaise's. That was no change. That was replacement. It was no longer the church she knew. A conjuror's trick. Pouf! Gone, and in its place, something else. She neither liked it (as she had liked her four-century-old church) nor disliked it. She felt a little more at ease inside the church, however. They had maintained the same old gilded, ornate altar. Yes it was her St. Blaise's, all right.

She visualized the scene outside the church: Caesar

Road, that asphalt artery that ran from Amboli naka through Kevni and then Amboli village, past Andrew D'mello's Doris Terrace to join the Andheri-Versova Road. She remembered it as it was in the mid-1940s, when her family had moved to these parts, a narrow tarred strip, as much a footpath as village highway for bullock carts, the occasional hossgary (that Anglo-Marathi translation of ghoda gaadi or horse carriage) and very rarely a motor vehicle. Pedestrian, vehicle, carriage and cart gave way to each other in response to yells and, at times, that impolite new sound: the motor horn. Feast Day cuisine roamed the streets cluck-quack-grunting their promise of kuddi, moile and sorpotel, the chickens and ducks having learnt when to cross the street; the pigs luxuriating in the slush of the gutters on both sides of Caesar Road. The gutters took preference over the need for pavement space and served as Kevni-Amboli's poultry farm and piggery.

Caesar Road was asterisked with reminiscences for Kitty. At the entrance, where the road met the main S.V. Road (originally Ghodbunder Road) the police chowki stood to attention as you turned the corner. Modestly constructed of asbestos on wooden strips, it served more as a phone booth than as police junction. It housed the only phone in the neighbourhood for many years, and of course a havildar who slept all day with eyes half open. To hell with those village boys for whom a rollicking fight was adult lollipop. Let them bash each other for mutual punishment and reward; let them be their own police for all he cared.

Kitty remembers: she was just ten then. She and her mother had gone to the chowki to make an urgent telephone call. The door was partially shut. Her mother pushed it open to find, to her shock and embarrassment, our havildar with his fly open and his navy blue short pants half lowered. With a thick needle and thread, borrowed from the mochi, he was trying to sew on a button, those being pre-zipper days. The sudden appearance of two females was startling and left, to say the least, policeman and needle quite shaken. The needle's point totally missed the button. The two intruders saw the man grimace while he let out a painful '*aaiieee*,' followed by a '*chi-kit-kit*,' which we will politely render as 'Ouch!' Kitty and her mother sped homeward lest they be booked for assaulting a policeman.

More asterisks. Down the road, a few metres away on the right, Kevni village had received its first gift from the new municipality—a public tap in place of the old well. There was much jubilation and pride among the housewives of the chawl opposite the new installation; a sense of having arrived at the threshold of modernity; no more straining of those womanly muscles to draw water from depths that could, in the hot months of April, May and June, be punishing. The ladies took their brass and copper handas, now polished to a respectful shine, and

walked with an exaggerated sway to the new tap. It didn't
take them long to realize that while the circumference of
their old well, now covered with mud, stones and cement,
could have ten or more women draw water at the same
time, the stylish new tap demanded the discipline of a
queue, a silly one-person-at-a-time thing. The tap had
turned into a ration shop. Water was released at fixed times,
so patience and time were at a premium. The ladies started
coming to the tap with as many handas as they could, each
keeping the queue waiting while they filled all of them.
Tap-water time was a concert of shrill voices, in which you
may pick out some choice feminine abuse in Marathi. The
belligerence was not always verbal. Kitty, not yet in her
teens, was witness to one time when two ladies confronted
each other, one grabbing hold of the other's hair. The other
ladies stood and egged them on till it became apparent that
this was going to be a fight to the finish; those womanly
muscles hardened by years of drawing water now proved
good for the new ways of fetching water. Claws dug into
each other's cheeks till they bled. On that wet, uneven
surface, the two fell to the ground and were soaking wet
before they could rise to continue their determined claw
fencing. Before they knew it, they were tearing at each
other's clothes; first one then the other choli was ripped
open, baring braless breasts. The stronger of the two was
now intent on stripping the other naked. Kitty, unable to
just stand and watch, rushed unthinkingly to try and stop

them when a saner hand from the queue held her back. No one tried to stop the fight. Some men too collected to watch. The fight would only finish with the complete stripping of the weaker of the two women, who sobbed with shame when the final shred of her gagra had fallen. She tried to hide her breasts with her hands and sat on her haunches to protect the other end of her modesty. Just then Bertha from Everest Lane was returning from the market. Bertha was one of those who walked with her head lowered, looking neither left nor right, yet when she passed by someone she knew, it was as if she sensed the person's presence, and she looked up, smiled, and gave him or her the time of day. In her early twenties, Bertha was slim and petite, with a gentle face which Kitty often admired. Seeing what was happening, she stopped, looked at the scene for a minute or two. She kept her bag down, went up to the naked woman and gently led her across the street to the chawl. At the same time, the husband of the stronger woman was seen striding angrily towards his wife, who herself was half-naked. Without a word, he grabbed her by her hair and dragged her across Caesar Road to their home in the chawl.

More asterisks, big, small, old and more recent popped up in Kitty's head as she mentally walked down Caesar Road: she remembered when the road was St. Blaise's School's annual sports ground. The 50-metre sprint started from the church entrance and ended at Mr. Mendonca's house; 100 metres up to Rita Villa and 500 metres to the Croft.

And then that terrible fire in the Amboli mutton shop, which was set ablaze allegedly by the newly formed ultra right-wing Shiv Sena during what turned out to be a mini riot between communal groups in Amboli. It was ugly. To Kitty, a little older by this time, a college student, the incident was disturbing and left a scar on her sensitivities.

It was a little after dusk when a group of marauders surrounded the mutton shop, drenched it with kerosene and set it on fire. Fortunately, there was nobody inside but six or seven goats were trapped in the blaze. Kitty wept, as did many grown men, when they heard the pitiful bleating of the animals; a sound that, to her, was more heart-rending than the sound of a child crying. She felt sinful, she said, as she stood there doing nothing—partly because she, and so many others, had seen the police van standing a little beyond Doris Terrace and thought that it would rush to the rescue. But the van seemed glued to where it was, the policeman watching the scene until the deed was done and the miscreants had fled. When they finally decided to drive over and enter the charred shop, Kitty made bold to go and confront the police. Mr. Rebello pulled her back and told her not to do anything foolish. As she moved away from the scene with Mr. Rebello, she heard the chortling of the policemen. She heard one of them say, 'Fuss kilass mutton re. Thailee anlaa ka?' Perhaps it was at this point, her first confrontation with the partisan nature of the police, that Kitty took a decision with regard to her career.

The asphalt artery had thickened over the years and had become clogged with carbon monoxide-belching vehicles. It conceded narrow strips at the sides of the road as apologies for pavements, as the pigs, ducks and chickens slowly faded out. A few old cottages on either side were swallowed up by multistoreyed monstrosities, villainously thumbing their noses at history and aesthetics.

Yes, Kitty acknowledged, there *was* Change.

Looking down again at the coffin now, she knew she was looking at a different person from the Hanging Gardens of fifty years ago. After his mother's death, the St. Vincent de Paul Society had had him admitted into the Old Age Home at Chakala. Earlier, they had arranged to have his hernia and hydrocele surgically attended to. Hanging Gardens was no longer Hanging Gardens. He was, as stated on his coffin cover and in the obituary in the *Times of India* that day, Joseph Anthony Miranda, son of Francis Miranda.

But funerals always take you back.

Kalaripayattu

Back fifty. The day Kitty foiled that mischievous scrotum-teasing bid by Cliffy and Dominic. Her mother, Cecilia, was secretly proud of her daughter's bravery against the bullies. Little as she was, Kitty had a sense of justice and a feeling for the underdog, she thought to herself as she embroidered in her mind a story that she could present to her younger Byculla sisters when they visited her the next week. She patted her daughter on the head and said, 'You must be careful with these big boys, baby. They are stronger than you, you know.'

Just then, there was a knock on the door. The door (as always, and in most homes in Kevni's chawls) was open to let in light, air and good company. At the door stood Dominic displaying a surgical plaster on his temple. He was accompanied by his mother, hands menacingly on hips, and flamethrowers for eyes.

Before she had set out on this intentionally belligerent visit, she had worked herself up to a rage at home, ranting about these outsiders, these Goans and Mangaloreans, junglees who come here to spoil our village, to distil liquor and spoil our husbands. 'More and more are coming,' she moaned to her husband, 'like cockroaches. They will soon throw us out, you will see. Look how they beat up our son,' she continued her moaning. Blaise, her husband, could not agree more. 'Bleddy chawlees. No toopice in pocket and they lagao perfume and do their conkrekonk! But this Kitty girl is not even Goan, menn. Some yanda-goondoo bhel-puri.'

As she stood at Cecilia's threshold, she was determined to confront these people. Eyes ablaze, she said to Kitty's mother, 'Look what your daughter done to my son! Look, no! Look!'

'My God!' Cecilia exclaimed, looking aghast. 'I didn't know it was so bad. I'm so sorry. Is it hurting you, baba?'

'No. Not at all, auntie,' said Dominic before his mother could interrupt. 'Nothing. No hurt at all.'

'Who told you to open your mouth?' his mother snapped at him, her hand raised for a slap. She held back and said, '*Ghari za tu ata.* Go home stupid you … '

Shrewdly picking up from the boy's foot-in-mouth, Cecilia said, 'I'm happy Dominic is not hurt. And now at least he will not do such a bad thing again.'

'Nonsense you talk. Your chintoo-pintoo daughter is not going to teach my son anything, you hear? Throwing stones! You outsiders must learn to behave if you want to live here.'

'Come in,' Cecilia said by way of a charm offensive. 'Have a cup of Mangalorean coffee.'

'I don't want your coffee-toffee nonsense,' said our rhyming East Indian as she walked away.

That evening when Kitty's father, George Thomas, came home from work, his response to the episode was muted. He took his daughter gently by the hand and sat her down next to him on the rexine-clad sofa.

'Were you angry with Cliffy and Dominic?'

'Yes, Daddy.'

'And you picked up a stone to throw at them?'

'Yes, Daddy.'

'Why?'

'To stop what they were doing. They were hurting Hanging Gardens. They pulled his pants down. And everyone then could see his bibi.'

'You were right in wanting to stop them. But …'

'But what, Daddy?'

George paused. Speaking slowly, he said, 'It is alright this time, but I want you to think about what I am going to tell you.'

Kitty got up from the sofa and sat down on the floor. It was easier to see her father's face from down there. George spoke slowly, now suddenly unsure of what he wanted to tell his daughter.

'It's not nice to throw stones, Kitty baby. Good people do not throw stones; only cowards do it,' he said. 'It is not nice to hurt people.' He paused. He had a feeling that he was not saying it right. 'But sometimes, like today, when you have to, you … Oh … forget it, Kitty,' he stopped abruptly, realizing that he wasn't making sense even to himself. 'I will tell you about it some other day.'

'Why not now, Daddy?'

'You are a little girl now, baby. And…'

'Yes, Daddy?'

'… it is not nice for girls to fight.'

'I was not fighting. I just wanted to make Cliffy and Dominic stop what they were doing,' she said.

They spoke English, the only language common to all three. Cecilia was a Mangalorean (a Monteiro), most comfortable with Konkani, which she used with her side of the family. Kitty's father was a Keralite, what the village folk called a 'yanda-goondoo'. He couldn't speak Konkani and she didn't know Malayalam. So, English it was between them. Whatever English they knew. As a result, Kitty got her English in two wildly differing accents at home, which in time she would filter through the more 'English'-sounding English that she picked up from some of her better-spoken teachers such as Miss Flavia, Miss Alice and Miss Doris.

The confusion of George's caution interruptus of that day stayed like a teasing mirage in Kitty's mind for years. It was resolved for her in an episode she would never forget.

Kevni village was staging a concert. Hand-made

posters were displayed everywhere. The Sutaris, Pereiras and Gonsalveses were putting together an East Indian extravaganza. The stage was set up in the rough and stony quadrangle in front of Pascoal Pereira's house, bordered on the left and right by two chawls. Left of the stage and a little behind it was a deep well that was rarely used, now that the municipality had given the village a couple of public taps.

That evening, every single home in Kevni was locked up and empty. They were all attending the concert. The quadrangle was full to overflowing. Chairs were ordered for prominent villagers and for the elderly. The others brought their own seats: stools, old tea chests and Dalda dabbas. The chawl residents and their friends could watch from their homes.

It was a spectacular show. Performances by pucca East Indians like Victor Sutari, Nancy and Braz drew wild applause for their robust rendering of especially composed East Indian 'numbers'. The lively koli and kunbi dances, with their colourful costumes and backdrops, had everybody clamouring for more. Palms sore from clapping were testimonials of a great show.

And then it started happening: a timed drizzle of pebbles. Subdued ouches were heard from the middle rows, then from the front seats. Yet they sat, refusing to be distracted from the evening's entertainment. The pandemonium began when Victor Sutari, in the middle of his second verse, was struck by a small rock on his forehead and knocked down on the stage.

At that moment someone cried, 'Pakad thyala! Catch the bastard!'

Eyes turned towards the left of the stage, near the well, where Phineas, Sabby, the Castro chap and a couple of others were holding onto a short, slim young fellow not yet in his twenties. Torchlight was shone on the scene. Instant recognition. 'It's Tony from Amboli village!' There was a scuffle as Tony managed to slip from their grasp and started to run, chased by an excited group. He tripped over a loose stone slab. Someone caught hold of his ankle as he fell. He dragged himself forward towards the parapet of the well. In the push and shove, he found himself falling headlong over the rim and into the well. The crowd held its collective breath for a seeming eternity before they heard the splash. A loud whisper: 'He's dead!' The torchlight was shone down into the circular blackness. 'Not dead,' Phineas' voice was heard reverberating in the well. 'The buggar can swim, menn!'

Nobody knew how word got to the neighbouring Amboli village but within minutes, Tony's brother was seen charging into Kevni, leading a mini-army of Amboliites, all armed with bamboo sticks, iron rods and knuckledusters. It was all-out war. There could not have been more than ten Amboliites in what could be seen as hostile territory, but they came secure in their belief that the Kevniite was a maamiya, a softy, a coward who didn't even know that he had two useful fists, a belief that was confirmed that day as knuckleduster and rod found their mark on Kevni's half-hearted warriors. Bloody noses and broken jaws were seen slinking away into their homes as Amboli gave Kevni a good thrashing.

Kitty, holding onto her father's hand, watched from a corner. They saw Kevni's Castro pick up a big rock. He was aiming to hurl it at one of the Amboli gang. 'No!' George shouted as he darted forward, in time to stop the stone from being thrown. He pushed Castro aside, looked back at Kitty and said, 'You stand there. Don't move.' Quickly and with his face expressionless, he did a flying leap to where the action was at its fiercest, executing a horizontal spin in the air at about head level, legs spread-eagled to catch two or three jaws with his shoes. The Ambolis didn't know what had hit them. As he landed on the ground, he intercepted a stout bamboo stick that was being brought down by an Amboliite on Ignatius' back, snatched it with both hands and spun it around like a fan in all directions. You could hear the crack of bamboo on bone with every turn of the stick. At least four boys were on the ground, groaning with pain, while the others seemed paralyzed as George did another aerial spin.

At about the same time, on the first floor of Doris Terrace, Amboli's Patsy D'mello got the news that the village boys had gone to Kevni to 'give those buggars a pasting.' He was furious. 'Idiots!' he said. 'Do they always have to go looking for trouble?' He quickly dressed and set off at a run.

At six-foot-three, Patsy towered above the entire Amboli cricket team, not just in height, but also in the regard with which he was held. When he walked to the cricket crease, bat in hand, the field resounded with a chorus of 'Patsy! Patsy! Patsy!' A swing at the very first ball and it would sprout wings, it seemed, as spectators watched it soar above the tadgola tree for a six. And then another. And another. To crescendos of that one-word chorus: 'Patsy!!' In church, his controlled, resonant tenor lent a refined timbre to the attempted polyphony of the parish choir. To St. Blaise's parishioners Patsy was a well-read intellectual, a musician and a person not to be trifled with. Yet he chose to mingle with the youth of the village, many of whom were no more than unlettered mimics of cowboy movie heroes, practising their left-uppercuts and jabs in front of a mirror or on some weak and vulnerable looking bystander. Patsy was looked up to as cricket captain, mentor and leader.

'I'll teach our boys a lesson,' he said. 'Drag them back by their ears and give them a bloody hiding.' But when he reached the scene of warfare, he was greeted by a sight he had never expected to see. He found four or five of his boys groaning on the ground. He saw a slim dark fellow end an aerial spin that knocked a few more of his boys down. A loose-limbed Kevni twit who could be blown away by a sneeze was trying to kick one of the Amboli boys who was struggling to stand up when the slim dark fellow stopped him. 'Don't!' he commanded. 'Can't you see he's down?'

Patsy, who had come to take his boys back home, was in half a mind to sock that slim dark fellow on the jaw for all the damage he had done, but something in the man's demeanour stopped him from doing so. He turned one of the fallen boys over. It was Tony's brother, bleeding from his nose and mouth.

'I have two broken teeth and my nose is cracked,' he told Patsy.

'Come home,' said Patsy, as he lifted the boy over his shoulders like a sack of potatoes. 'I'm going to break two more for you, you duffer.'

The next morning, a representative group of Amboliites visited the home of George Thomas accompanied by Tony's mother.

They came straight to the point. 'Why don't you come and stay in Amboli? We bleddy want you for us.'

'I will give you a room in my chawl,' Tony's mother offered. 'Less rent you can pay.'

'But why? I'm happy here.'

'We bleddy want someone like you.'

'How nice you fight, menn?'

'Like in the bleddy pichers, no?'

'On Good Friday, the Gundowli buggars will be coming to our church for the passo. We want to give them a bleddy pasting. We want you to do fighting for us.'

George looked at them for a long time. He laughed. 'I don't fight,' he said.

'But you fought with us, menn. See you broke my nose. See!'

'I was not fighting,' he said quietly.

'Then what?'

'I came to stop the fighting. And I think I did,' he told them with the hint of a smile.

In the years that followed, Kitty gleaned the answers to some of the questions she was not able to frame as a little girl. They came from her father's casual comments, from his quiet conversations with her and with her mother, from his unflappability in the face of provocation or panic, and from the sense she got of his inner resolve. Realization trickled in that what she was witnessing in her father's way of life had something to do with the way he fought on that day.

'Did you have to learn how to fight like that?'

'Yes,' he told her. 'I had to learn *not* to fight first. Only then they would teach me how to fight.'

'Who taught you?'

'My kalaripayattu masters.'

'Kalaripayattu?'

'It's a very old martial art of South India from where I come. But it is more than fighting.'

Over the following years, as she slid into her teens, the questions kept coming for George. His answers came slowly, through a very fine sieve: that of his life as an orphan in Kerala, where he and his twin brother were brought up in an institution that cared for children like him. He was sent to school where he did well enough to pass his SSC examination with good marks. Simultaneously, he and his brother were picked for kalaripayattu training, which was imparted by the school principal himself.

The twins got to be so good that they were called upon to give demonstrations of kalaripayattu at various cultural functions, on stage and sometimes for five-star hotels as entertainment. Often they travelled across Kerala to do these performances for which they got paid. They demonstrated hand-to-hand combat, kalaripayattu with sticks, swords and flexible metal strips. Their principal later put a stop to it. They could not be doing this for the rest of their lives. They had to do something else for a living. He encouraged them to go to college and complete their graduation—both of them in science. It was not long before his brother, Matthew, got himself a job in Dubai, whereas George came to Bombay, met his wife-to-be and got married.

'Teach me kalaripayattu,' Kitty begged of her father, but he would pass off the request with a smile.

Kitty was persistent. 'Is it because I am a girl?' she asked.

'No,' he told her. 'I know girls who are very good at the art, though not many.'

'Then why won't you teach me?'

'What will you do with it? You have no need for kalaripayattu today,' he said and knew at once that he had trapped himself.

'But I have seen you using kalaripayattu. It was needed then, wasn't it?'

'Kalaripayattu is not easy. You need a strong mind and a lot of determination.'

'Do you think I do not have a strong mind, Daddy?'

'You have to learn to think kalaripayattu before you practice it.'

'I am ready to learn,' she told him.

Learning was easy, practice was not. Not so much the techniques of combat as the control of thoughts and the reining in of emotions: anger management, the resolve never to fight, to know when fighting was needed, and in those rare cases when it would be needed, never to fight in anger, because anger would consume the energy needed for combat. Fighting (bad word, that) had to be in direct contact with the assailant—body to body, or at worst via another body, animate or inanimate, such as a stick or sword, if the assailant was similarly armed; never resort to missiles such as stones or bullets—the weapons of cowards and weaklings.

In time, she picked up the basics of kalaripayattu: the attitudes, the movements, the steps and the grace of that art. She and her father would wake up every day before dawn and walk to the fields behind Valentine Matthew's vegetable farm, where the boys had flattened out a cricket pitch for their evening game. There, in silhouette against the rising sun, father and daughter could be seen doing what seemed like a strenuous dance; perfecting their chuvadu, vadivu, prayogam, anthakari and the many fine movements of kalaripayattu. Her mother would notice that as their daughter got more adept, she became less aggressive and more quick-witted. Her lively wit replaced the flying fist as a response to the boys' 'Kitty-Kitty-tomboy-half-girl-half-boy' chant. But tomboy she always remained, ready to join in a game of marbles, tops, kite-flying and even cricket.

Once, when the Kevni team was short of a player in a match against Amboli, she offered to be the eleventh player. Even as last 'man' in, she was able to score the needed ten runs with two fours. It helped win the match, much to Kevni's later regret. Forever after that the Kevni team was labelled by Amboli as the GCC. 'The Girlie Cricket Club'…

Funny, the things you remember at a funeral.

Today standing with the others around the body of Hanging Gardens, Kitty remained expressionless as the episodes played out vividly in her memory.

Apart from herself and the officiating priest, there were only four other persons present at this quiet, emotionless funeral. One of them was Cliffy, now balding and quite grey. He was there with his wife, Hazel.

Bastiao

The punitive belt laid aside, Cliffy's father, Bastiao ('Pai' to Cliffy) went down on his knees in front of their little altar and begged a silent forgiveness, a 'somya kakut kor', for what he had just done to his son. He prayed too that his Cliffy baba would grow up to be a good boy and not do what he did that day.

Up from his knees, he spoke to his son, with a glance at his wife too. 'Just because a family has come down in life is no reason for us to be unkind to them.' They spoke Bardez Konkani at home. In the village, it was whatever English they could manage. 'Be kind to that poor man, baba,' he said in a tone that was meant to be balm to the hurt he had just inflicted on his son. He made as if to put an arm around the boy, but held back at the last moment.

Bastiao Rodricks was what the predominantly East Indian villagers recognized as a non-interfering, 'god-fearing' man, a perception that helped to barely acquit him of his offence of being an outsider, a bleddy Goan.

He was seen in church every morning attending two Masses and kissing every statue before he headed home. Piety with invisibility was what helped you to get at least partially accepted in the villages of Kevni and Amboli. He had come to the Bombay of the late 1930s as a young man with nothing but his rebekk—his violin that helped brighten up his empty moments—and a small tin trunk which contained his belongings. He had moved into one of those kudds in Dhobi Talao, paying a rupee every month for his lodging that he shared with so many others from his village. He had to find work to earn a living, the reason for his leaving his comfortable home in Goa and coming to this city. He was an expert coconut-plucker and toddy-tapper in his village of Mandrem, but they had no use for those rare skills here in the asphalt shores of his adopted city. He figured that tailoring made more sense in a city where even an office clerk had to wear a necktie. He took up a job as a tailor's assistant, where he quickly picked up the craft of scissors and tailors' chalk.

A marriage proposal sent him scurrying back to Goa. An engagement ring, a quick wedding celebration and a small dowry later, he happily settled down and thought about what to do with his life from then on.

He could not go back to the kudd with his new bride. He had to look for a small rented dwelling place for himself and his wife. He looked at rooms in areas that had predominant clusters of Goan Catholics. His search, which began in the small lanes around the Fort area, crept northward towards Dhobi Talao, Girgaon, Mazagon, Parel, Dadar's Salvação parish and Mahim. All of them were way beyond the reach of his inflexible rupee; all of them looking for that 'goodwill money' called pugri. Even his wife's dowry, generous though in intention, was a smidgen in relation to the asking amount. He had to look further north, in the suburbs, for a place to call home.

The real estate tide of those days brought him to distant Andheri, where again there seemed nothing to suit his pocket until he came to the East Indian-dominated villages of Kevni, Amboli and Ossorem. The local landlords, seeing opportunity, had constructed temporary structures of bamboo held together by mud. (Some of these 'temporary' structures are being occupied even to this day.) These were long tenements. Chawls, they were called, but quite unlike the brick-and-mortar multi-storeyed chawls of the city. Each chawl was a line of about eight to ten small 10ft x 10ft one-room homes. A bamboo wall separated one home from another, permitting you the favour of just visual privacy; your bedroom whispers, broadcast across to at least two families on either side of your home, enabled your neighbours to predict your wife's delivery date even before your gynaecologist. Truly *these* walls had ears. The floors were smeared with cowdung, which they were told had antiseptic properties, kept mosquitoes and flies away and were good for the family health. Within each room there was a 2ft x 2ft cemented space which could be used for washing clothes, scrubbing vessels and for a bath if you could enclose the space with a curtain and if you could manage enough water for the purpose. There usually was a common outdoor tap for all the tenants and one or two shared outdoor lavatories.

Bastiao looked at these and was on the verge of taking one of the chawls in Kevni when he was shown a couple of others which were of the same design, but constructed out of brick and cement. These cost three rupees more per month than the bamboo-and-mud variety. A good ten rupees would then go from his monthly income of ninety rupees as tailor's assistant. He would also have to take into account his train pass from Andheri to Churchgate, his place of work. He decided to pay the three rupees more and cut down on something else.

God was good to him, he said. Things worked out right. He was able to buy a sewing machine on instalments and start his own tailoring business from his home. He specialized in shirts and the orders kept coming in. Life was not bad after all. God had blessed him with a good wife. And a good son. At least that's what he told himself all these years.

And then, today, he had to catch him doing this sinful thing…

He turned to face Cliffy, who was still smarting from that hateful belt.

'Come,' he said. 'Let's go.'

'Where are you taking him?' his wife asked.

'To Anton's house.'

'Anton?'

'Anton Miranda. Hanging Gardens.'

'But why?'

'Come.' He said to his son again, not bothering to answer his wife. Cliffy followed his father obediently.

Hanging Gardens' home was a little more than a sickly swelling behind the joint family house of the Misquittas. Constructed out of loose, irregular-shaped rocks put together with spit and mud, it would seem the house could barely take the height of an adult. Hanging Gardens' mother, Carmine, could stand comfortably, but her son had to stoop a little to avoid knocking over their thatched roof. The house, now a good ten years old, was put together in just two days for Carmine, who at that time had been employed by the Misquittas to do their 'top work', the sweeping, swabbing, laundry and washing of vessels.

Through a small opening in the wall, where a few rocks had been left out as an apology for a window, a ray of dusty light played on the features of Carmine's face. In the gloomy dimness of the room, her face looked like an old photograph, black and white with a hint of sepia. Liquor and ten hard years may have robbed that face of some of its fleshy moulding, rendering it gaunt, a little angular, but there was no sign of wrinkles. Dark, smooth skin stretched a little loosely over features which, in that one-sided lighting, seemed to Bastiao close to stunning: a classic nose, slightly generous lips and a subtly divided chin. Her hair, wavy, almost curly, needed some tending, but showed no signs of greying yet. She must have been quite a looker when she was younger, Bastiao thought, and quickly brushed the image from his mind lest it bring on sinful thoughts that might need confession the next Saturday. Her son, Anton, with his crude, podgy face had clearly taken after his father, not his mother.

Bastiao and his son stood by the open door. Carmine was sitting on the cowdung floor, resting against the wall, knees folded up in front of her. She was wearing what must have once been an expensive and attractive dress, and which now needed much darning and washing. She had a small collection of some of the most fashionable dresses in that tin trunk of hers, the sartorial discards of the Misquittas, Gomeses, Pereiras and the other kind ladies who donated to the St. Vincent de Paul Society.

She did not stand to receive her guests; just looked up and asked: 'What do you want?'

'Our son has come to say sorry to your son.' Bastiao spoke in Konkani.

'Anton is not at home. What did your son do?' Carmine answered in English.

'He was teasing your son.'

'Everybody teases my son. No need to say sorry.'

'He even hurt him with a stick.' Bastiao said softly, as if in a confessional.

Carmine turned to Cliffy and said, 'Why baba? Why do you do these things? My son Anton does no harm to anyone.' Then turning to Bastiao, 'His only sin is the sin of his birth. My sin. We gave him bussa instead of a brain.'

Sawdust instead of a brain. Bastiao felt fresh guilt for his son's casual cruelty. As his eyes got used to the darkness, Bastiao saw a few clothes hanging on a cord. There was a mud platform with a wood-fire chula. Sitting on it was a pot blackened with soot. Leaning against it were two misshapen tin plates. The ashes of the chula were spread out all over the floor. There were two old rusty trunks which served as storage and seating. An old violin case stood against the wall.

'Does someone play the violin?' Bastiao asked.

'Anton's father used to,' she said with a sigh. 'There's no violin in it now. I sold it years ago. There are only old photographs inside. Anton's father's pictures.'

On the wall opposite the entrance was a huge photo frame with the portrait of a distinguished-looking gentleman. His long, meticulously groomed sideburns were continuous with a huge moustache, but no beard. He was obviously a person who worked on his looks. There was no doubt in the way the picture was taken that the gentleman was a very important person.

'Who's that?' Bastiao asked.

'That's Anton's father's grandfather. Famous doctor, first in Portugal, then in Goa. Big man. But what's the use. Look where his great-grandson is! I don't know why I keep that big frame in my house. I should sell it and get some money. That big man is not going to feed me.' She stopped speaking and looked towards the door. 'There he is, Anton.'

Hanging Gardens became Anton to all present the moment he entered the house, stooping to get through the door. Bending all the way, he sat down on the floor next to his mother. The two guests were seated on the tin trunks.

Carmine said to him. 'Your friends have come.'

Anton stared at Cliffy, pointed a finger at him and said in Hindi, 'Mara mereko.' Turning to his mother, he said in Marathi, 'Marla mala.'

'Sorry bolaila ala,' she said.

'Sorry munn, re,' Bastiao ordered his son.

'Sorry,' said Cliffy, as if he was just learning the word.

'Borem bashen munn, re.' Bastiao said sternly. 'Say it properly.'

'I am sorry,' Cliffy said a little louder and in English, looking at Anton. This time it sounded like he meant it.

There was a moment of silence. Anton scratched his dishevelled head with a bored expression. He dipped his hand into his shirt pocket and took out a one-rupee note, his earnings for the day, and handed it to his mother. 'Tula,' he said. His hand went into his pocket again and came out with a 'bull's-eye', one of those black-and-white striped hard mentholated candies popular among children. He offered it to Cliffy. 'Tula,' he said with no expression.

At the funeral today, Cliffy looked across at the other side of the coffin, where Kitty was standing, lost, it would seem, in profound thought. Next to him were the two gravediggers, Bhiku and Janardhan, standing with their hands joined reverently in front of them. It needed just one of them for the job, but both insisted on doing it as a tribute to their senior grave-digging comrade. Hanging Gardens had stopped digging graves at least a decade ago and so had they. Today's digging, they told the vicar, was their panegyric for their partner.

Cliffy was not listening to the prayers being intoned blandly by the priest. He looked at Hanging Gardens lying there in his coffin and his own lips shaped a silent 'Sorry' to a face that seemed to have more expression, he thought, than when he had said that word fifty years ago.

Misquitta

Hanging Gardens' destiny was as incoherent as his speech. He stumbled into grave-digging as a job in his mid-twenties. Till then he was everyone's handyman. From schoolboys to landlords, they ordered him around and he seemed glad to be able to do what he figured the others couldn't.

His first grave-digging assignment was a piece of local history.

It had to do with the Misquitta family, the people to whom his mother and he were beholden. The two-storeyed Misquitta house, painted regularly every two years before Christmas, was a landmark in Kevni. The painting would start without exception on the 1st of October every other year, the contractor and his painters having to report for duty at 8.30 on that morning, when paterfamilias Blaise Misquitta would give them a meticulous schedule of work, written down to the minute—their time of arrival every morning and the time to stop work every evening.

He would give them a neat hand-made chart of when he expected them to start and finish each room, allowing time for scraping, plastering and three coats of paint. There were twelve rooms, a large living room, kitchen and two bathrooms in the two-storeyed building, not counting four balconies. They had to commit to strict deadlines or else the contractor would have to pay penalties for each delay. This, he explained to his neighbours, was necessary or everything else in the home would go topsy-turvy for months. It worked beautifully for him.

But that's how Blaise Misquitta did everything. He was driven by the hands of his old grandfather clock. He abhorred unpunctuality, counting it as one of the mortal sins of the Catholic community. 'Why are you never on time?' he would ask. 'I would rather you be an hour early than a minute late,' he would say.

Just five-feet-four-inches in height, Mr Misquitta was a standing testimony to his favourite saying that stature was not measured in feet and inches. His name at the head of a number of church groups, and the Pro Ecclesia et Pontifice awarded to him by the Pope and displayed prominently in his living room at a decent enough distance from the altar of the Sacred Heart, were only some of the manifestations of his standing in Kevni. As far as his knowledge went, there was only one other person to be so awarded—Joe D'mello of Amboli. Good man, Joe. Misquitta had fathered seven children from two wives and at last count had four grandchildren. The studio photograph on the mantelpiece of nineteen family members around this great little personage was his certificate of heaven's blessing and testimony of his prestige, not to speak of his virility.

His penchant for punctuality was legendary. How could anyone forget the wedding of his first son? The bridegroom and his best man were at the entrance of St. Michael's Church, Mahim, a good twenty-one minutes before 8.30 a.m., the time fixed for the nuptials to begin. The bride, who was from Mahim parish, was just a two-minute drive from the church by hired car. On the dot of 8.30, Daddy Misquitta pulled out his silver pocket watch. You could see his jaw muscles tighten. At 8.31 he walked briskly onto the main road, looked up and down the street to see if he could spot the bridal car. He came back, looking frighteningly stern. The bride was now three minutes late. He waited two more minutes before he told his son loudly enough for the congregation to hear, 'Call it off, son. This girl is not for you.' He then strode briskly to the sacristy where the officiating priest and the altar boys were dressed and ready.

'Forget it, Father. This wedding is off,' he said.

'Why? What happened?' Father D'souza asked in consternation.

'What happened, you ask! Can't you see? She is already seven minutes late.'

Father D'souza laughed and said, 'Don't be silly, Mr Misquitta, she'll be here now.'

Misquitta was fuming. '*I don't want her here now*. If she has no respect for the sacrament, what respect will she have for me?' Then added, 'And for her husband?'

The angry father walked up and down the sacristy once. 'It's off, Father. It's off, I'm telling you.'

That's when Father D'souza raised his voice. 'Don't be an imbecile.' It was probably the first time that someone had spoken to this Pro Ecclesia et Pontifice recipient in this tone.

'What? Father!' Misquitta couldn't believe his ears.

'The Church and I are asking you to have a little patience. It's a virtue greater than punctuality.'

Just then, the best man came in with the news that the bridal train was now in the church. He had already kissed the bride and she was walking now towards the bridal pew.

Nine minutes late!

Throughout the nuptials and the Mass, Misquitta stood with his arms crossed over his three-piece suit, eyes threatening to incinerate an entire congregation that saw nothing wrong with a transgression as serious as this. Whether they did or did not, every single person in the church that morning went back with a story that became a perennial winner as gossip and social banter, good for jaw-dropping shock and hearty guffaws. And of course it burnished to a glinting finish the reputation of Blaise Misquitta as a stickler for punctuality.

Six months later, when his second son and his best

man stood at the entrance of St. Peter's, Bandra, the entire congregation of invitees and parishioners released the collective breath they had been holding for the past two minutes, loud enough to drown the first few bars of the organist's Bridal March. Two minutes prior to this amplified sigh, on the dot of 8.28 a.m., our paterfamilias had ordered his son not to wait for the best man's kiss and to proceed to the bridal pew in front of the nave. The nuptials would start at 8.30 a.m. sharp with or without the bride. They had not yet reached the pew when a blur of dazzling white was seen flying from the entrance of the church to where they were. It was the bride doing a desperate sprint to her appointed place followed by bridesmaids vainly trying to hook her gown behind her back. Panting, she knelt on the pew even before her bridegroom could reach it. 8.30 a.m. sharp. She had made it. Once there, the bridesmaids were able to finally hook together her gown at the back. Another bridesmaid rushed in with the crown and the veil and deftly put them in place. In all that excitement, nobody had noticed that they had not heard the usual tick-tock of the bride's high heels as she made her entrance. Nobody had noticed that the bride had come in barefoot. A minute later a flower girl was seen discreetly bringing in the shoes that our Cinderella had not had time to put on.

In all this, the reader may run away with the impression that Blaise Misquitta was an unfeeling human being. Far from it. He was generous. As prominent member of the

St. Vincent de Paul society and in his own capacity, he doled out the money for many a family's rations, clothes and occasionally groceries and other provisions. On an evening, particularly after the rosary at the cross during the month of May, he would distribute boiled chickpeas to all those who recited the rosary. He believed that if we pushed our children closer to the Church and the Catholic religion, the world would be a better place.

For him religion was what helped you do the *right thing*. Rectitude was everything. Rectitude became piety inside the nave of a church and a strict adherence to form outside it. The line between his religion and his regimen— between sin and bad manners—was slim, if it existed at all. Not keeping a promise or not knocking before you enter would be as much a sin as stealing or coveting your neighbour's wife. In his book, it merited the absolution of the confessional. As in his religion, there were venial and mortal sins and then, sacrileges. Being late bordered on sacrilege.

God had blessed him with a good family. Seven obedient children and a beautiful young wife. This was his second; his first wife having died after the fifth child was born. She had caught pneumonia and, within a fortnight, she was dead. It had shattered him when it happened but the reading of the scriptures to him by the parish priest and much spiritual counselling helped him accept the will of God.

His rectitude and sense of responsibility towards his children prompted him to marry within a year of his wife's demise. He realized that, competent as he was, he would not be able to give his children the soft, caring warmth of a mother. He had to get married soon for the sake of his children. His feel for rightness also provided him with the insight that he ought to marry a young woman who would live long and be strong enough to look after his five children and then some of her own, which he ought to give her. He knew where he would find such a girl. He looked north towards the village of Gorai, where a number of girls, having worked for a few years in well-to-do East Indian families, had acquired the knowledge and finesse required to run a home like his.

Fiona, the one he picked, had the whole village blinking in disbelief. They had never seen someone as stunningly beautiful as this girl, except in the movies. A little on the buxom side (which in fact at that time was considered the most desirable feature of a girl's good looks; small breasts and short hair being seen as unfeminine), Fiona had long, healthy hair and was of good feminine height, which made her an inch taller than her husband. She had a light wheatish complexion and brown eyes that lit up in company. 'Misquitta had better look sharp,' the ladies of the village whispered.

The wedding took place on Fiona's twenty-first birthday. Her fifty-one-year-old husband looked a proud man at the altar that day.

She gave him a son within ten months of their marriage. 'The old man couldn't wait,' said the village's old men, green to the gills with envy. 'But then how could he with a girl as luscious as that?' For Blaise Misquitta, it was heaven's will and favour, not the lust of his loins or the seductive powers of a fulsome bosom that made it happen.

But then nothing happened after that for years. A barren decade went by for Blaise and Fiona. Not that either of them was complaining because life in the Misquitta household had overnight become a whirligig of fun. Fiona had a good voice and sang English and Marathi songs with much gusto. She knew how to jive and taught her stepsons the steps and movements of a dance that was the rage at that time. Even her husband tried putting his two left feet to the test. She loved company and entertained a lot, winning praise for her traditional East Indian dishes. A house that had dragged its feet all these years into a premature old age was now pumped up with young blood; with the children's friends, mostly energetic young men, getting together regularly at the house.

It looked like there were no more babies in the making for Daddy Misquitta. 'What a waste of a nice young girl,' said the same dirty old tongues.

At the age of thirty, Fiona caught a virulent form of pneumonia. It happened after a rollicking picnic to Madh Island with her stepsons and their young male friends. They were caught in a sudden shower, which of course they enjoyed. They came home drenched to the bone. Two days later, the sniffles and a slight fever had them sending for the doctor. A week later Dr D'souza pronounced pneumonia.

Mr Misquitta was a worried man. 'How serious is it, Doctor?' he asked remembering how his first wife had gone.

'It's a pretty virulent form,' the doctor said. 'But she's young and strong. She will be able to fight it.'

Unfortunately, the pneumonia climbed to a dangerous peak within the next week. Her breathing was hard and painful. Fiona was delirious and spoke of angels and devils that could be seen in her room. There was talk of shifting her to a hospital, but finally it was settled that they would hire two nurses for the day and night. Oxygen and glucose were given to her at home.

On the sixteenth day, it began to look hopeless. Fiona was gasping for breath. She seemed to be suffering from excruciating pain. After an hour-long examination, Dr. D'souza finally told her husband that there was no hope. In fact, he thought that she might not last another day. Could be hours. In the meantime, he said he would give her something for her heart and he suggested that they rub her down with brandy. Immediately after the doctor left, Blaise Misquitta took out his unopened bottle of Napoleon Brandy and asked the nurse to keep rubbing her down with it as instructed.

The poor man was distraught. Visions of his first wife's death haunted him like the devil's own movie show, playing back in wicked slow motion the final excruciating moments of her passing. It didn't stop there. It played back to him the day of the funeral, when the 'Libera Me' and 'Dies Irae' having been sung and over and the priest having sprinkled holy water over the body, the gravedigger was still only halfway down the grave. There was a huge crowd at the funeral, all of Kevni, Amboli, Andheri and the neighbouring parishes present, together with his friends and relations from the city, everyone wanting to register their condoling presence before the great little man. As if the death was not enough, fate had to scourge him with this shameful delay. As the digging continued for the next forty-five minutes, he wept loudly, inconsolably, not knowing himself whether it was out of grief or anger.

At the condolence ceremony, as the people came to sympathize with him, it was he who said to them, 'I'm sorry.'

He would not let it happen again. He had to be prepared for all eventualities.

He looked at Fiona struggling for breath. It was 4.35 p.m. by his pocket watch. He dressed up, put on his sola topi and went straight to church to meet the parish priest. 'Father not home,' he was told. He would not be back that day and would return early the next morning in time for the first Mass. Misquitta went in search of the gravedigger who, he was informed, had gone to his village in Roha.

He was walking back home in a panic when he was struck by a brainwave. Hanging Gardens! Yes. He could ask the boy to do it for him.

He hurried back to the police chowki, the only place that had a telephone in those days. He made a call to Fernandes, the undertakers, and ordered the most expensive teak coffin. The inscription would just be: FIONA MISQUITTA. AGE: 30. There was no need to mention dates.

At least that was settled. He had made sure that there would be no delays at the funeral this time.

Back home, he entered the room where his wife was visibly fighting for breath. She seemed even worse than a few hours ago. He held back his sobs as he told the nurses to continue with the brandy rub. It was 7.47 p.m. when he left the room. He went directly to the living room, knelt down in front of the altar of the Sacred Heart and said three paternosters and three Aves. Then he signed himself with the cross and went to the dining table where the rest of the family was waiting for him to say the grace. Gloom, like a dark fog, covered the gathering around the table. They said the grace together but when the servants brought the dishes to the table, they knew they would not be able to eat any of them. One by one they stood up and left the table.

Misquitta went back to the sickroom and sat down on one of the chairs. That face, which he thought was the most beautiful in the world, was now the colour of smudged paper. Her eyes were half-open, showing only the whites, her shapely nostrils twisted upward by the tube that fed her oxygen; her long hair dishevelled on the pillow. Every now and again her back would arch upward from the bed as she struggled for her next breath. No, it was the end, he knew.

He sat there for hours watching his wife till his eyelids began to droop. The night nurse advised him to get some sleep. She was there to keep a watch and to rub her down with brandy. She would do just the palms of the hands and soles of the feet. Reluctantly he left the room.

He woke up at 5 a.m., brushed his teeth and went directly to the sickroom. His wife's eyes were shut. She was no longer breathing hard. She lay still, looking lifeless.

'Tell me,' he said to the nurse in a fearful whisper. 'Tell me. What's happening?'

'I'm feeling better, Blaise,' he heard his wife say softly. Her eyes were still shut. Slowly she opened them and smiled. 'Much better,' she said.

'I think she will be alright,' said the nurse. 'Her breathing and pulse rate are much better. Temperature is normal.'

'Thank God!' was all he could say.

At about 8.30 a.m. a group of ladies arrived at Misquitta House, all dressed in black, enquiring about the time of the funeral.

'What funeral?' Misquitta asked.

'Your wife's. The grave has been dug and we saw the coffin cover outside the church with her name on it.'

Before he could put together a sensible enough answer in his mind, he saw more men and women arrive with funereal expressions.

'It must have been all that brandy,' Misquitta meant to say to himself, but it came out louder than intended.

'Brandy?' someone asked.

The eldest son had come out by then. 'Go back home,' he told them 'somebody is playing some terrible mischief. Sorry. Go back home. Everything is OK.'

Within a month, Fiona was back to her normal self and a little over a year later, on her husband's sixty-first birthday, she was able to present him with another son, pumping up the man's confidence in his own libido and giving rise to a whispered chorus of voices singing the cuckold's song.

That was when Fernandes the undertaker shyly spoke in person to Misquitta. 'I know you didn't use the coffin,' he said. 'But you still have to pay me for it, you know.'

'Oh yes,' said our man, feeling sheepish. And then with a touch of humour: 'I promise I won't disappear just like that.'

But that's just what happened. Two days later Blaise Misquitta had a bad case of food poisoning. In thirty-six hours, he was dead. It became a police case and a postmortem had to be done. Fiona decided that the body would be taken from the morgue directly to the gravesite. The funeral time was set. The grave was ready on time. A huge crowd had collected at the grave, waiting for the hearse with the body. But the police have their own efficiencies.

The hearse arrived forty minutes late, while the hymn 'Lord I'm Coming Home' was being sung. Fiona was inconsolable. She knew that nothing would pain her husband more than the thought that he had arrived late for his own funeral.

The next day, when they put up the announcement for the Third Day, Seventh Day and Month's Mind Masses, Fiona was furious. The announcement read as follows: REQUIEM HIGH MASSES FOR THE LATE MR BLAISE MISQUITTA.

Angrily she took a pen and scratched out the word, 'LATE'.

It was Hanging Gardens who dug the grave, for which he refused to take any payment.

Funerals

Kitty was there at most funerals. People found that strange, particularly her friends. She attended the funerals of even people she did not know. She made it a point to stand in the condolence queue and shake hands with the mourners, looking intently into their eyes. Why, her friends asked her, was she so interested in dead people? Not dead people, she told them, it was the living that she went to see. You see them every day, don't you? They countered. Every day I *see* them. At funerals, I come to know them, she said.

But those were glib and slippery answers designed to avoid the potentially lengthy, convoluted and possibly uncomfortable explanations for her unusual choice of social engagement, involving as it did her personal curiosity, vicariousness, empathy, insight, amusement, and of late, as a writer and journalist, a sense of history. Kitty believed that funerals were the bookmarks of local mythology. Each of them, singly and in clusters, sketched out the character of individuals, families and communities and, in time, served as the markers of a slowly changing age.

Even as a little girl of ten, when she would go to funerals, she would register every moan, cry and gesture of the nearest relative and the most indifferent spectator. After coming back home, she would re-enact the event in which you might well be audience to comedy, classical tragedy, the theatre of the absurd or opera buffa: the remembrances of the dear departed's kindness, bravery and even intimate conjugal moments melodramatically narrated, sometimes in plaintive plainchant by a dear-not-yet-departed, sometimes as a dialogue between the dear departed and the not-yet as if expecting from the departed a response: *Remember darling how I came home with an upset stomach after that Murzello wedding and how you held me tight and...and then how you ... Oh darling, remember?* Which would bring on a wave of sniffles and sobs and the trumpets of noses being blown that made the rest of the story unnecessary.

In her early teens, Kitty began to do character portraits of families based on their funereal behaviour and then predict to a nicety what would be heard and seen at subsequent graveside events. The Misquittas, for instance, were different from the D'mellos, the D'Silvas or the Pereiras; the Sutaris different from the Gonsalveses or the D'Penhas. Again, one Misquitta family was not the same as the other. There were five Misquitta families in Kevni, each one with distinct funereal manners from which you could safely and quite accurately delineate their characters.

One of the Misquitta families presented deadpan (unfortunate description) faces around the coffin and the gravesite right up to the lowering of the casket and the covering of the grave. And for days after that they would be seen walking to their jobs as if still part of a cortege, gait and pace keeping time, it would seem, to the Dead March; head half bowed, eyes lowered, not wanting to make conversation with anyone.

Another Misquitta family was all propriety and decorum, as if in an international investiture ceremony: everyone standing immaculately dressed in mourning, in what seemed like pre-appointed places at the graveside and the condolence line; sticking out their fingers for dainty handshakes, heads appropriately inclined to one side and with a half-smile pasted on their faces when they said their soft thank-yous.

Another Misquitta family was all camaraderie, slapping you on your back, though with not too excessive an enthusiasm lest it seem an affront to the dead, and enquiring about your health and that of your family, and how you were doing in your job and noting what a lousy day it was, and thus making you swallow that nice little condolence line you had taken the trouble to practice before coming to the funeral.

The other Misquitta family was, of course, much melodrama and emotion, much general weeping and wailing and plaintive plainchant.

While doing a course in writing and journalism after her graduation in English Honours, Kitty was corroborating her hypothesis that villages, too, displayed distinct funereal behaviour. She posited that the distinction was so clear that if she passed by the cemetery during a funeral she could tell, within a minute or two, which village it was that was burying its dead. Kevni funerals were, as a general rule, personal, private, close-knit affairs, with the exception of the Misquittas at whose burials neighbours and friends clamoured to be seen as involved and helpful. Amboli funerals, on the other hand, were collective events, like cricket matches on their 'tank'. The whole village would at least try to be present, whoever it was who had died, and prominent Amboliites would almost take ownership of that day. Being present was more than just a gesture of village loyalty and commitment; it was a show of solidarity and strength.

Andheri was understated but liturgically immaculate. Boasting of four priests and three nuns from just one gauthan, Andheri funerals paid attention to form, rubrics and ritual; at least one of the priests would be present there to officiate and wield some ecclesial influence in heaven for the deceased. The distant village of Ossorem could be loud and even ostentatious, with brass bands and mountains of wreaths and bouquets. Being farther away from the church than the other villages, they needed to inflate their presence in the parish, and expected and demanded a certain level of service from the church staff. On one occasion, one of the mourners interrupted her moaning to ask the priest why the service was so short and demanded more prayers to be said. She had heard a longer prayer being said at an Andheri funeral. At an Ossorem funeral, Kitty was witness to an 'aunty' in a nauvari mourning sari suddenly turn on one of the attendees and deliver in Marathi a rather piquant plaintive plainchant: 'Are you happy now? He's dead. You can go and take that langoti piece of land for yourself. He will not need it up there in heaven, where you will never go.' That was the cue for more sobs, sniffles and nasal trumpeting.

Over time, Kitty observed that funerals had changed their character. This was expected with the villages themselves going through an evolution, some slower than the others. The generally flat contours of Kevni's character may not have shown any significant spikes, but Amboli was going through a transformation and it was not slow in manifesting itself. With the fist-happy boys now forced to take up whatever jobs they could, many of them qualifying because of their sports, the cricket stumps and hockey sticks used as weapons and the knuckledusters were kept aside. Sixers and forward passes replaced left uppercuts and *dishoom dishoom*. Their combative urges were channelled to the 'tank', where competitive matches were held on Sundays. They could still give the buggars a thrashing, but now it would be on the sports field. How much of this was due to the influence and leadership of their flagpole, Patsy D'mello, is not known but he certainly encouraged the change.

Underneath it all and somewhat quietly, another dimension of Amboli's personality was coming to the surface. A Hawaiian guitarist, Nicholas Gonsalves, who for some reason had been lying low for so many years, decided to wipe the dust off his instrument and wake the village up with the delicate glissando of his slide guitar. They woke up too to the chamber sounds of Doris Terrace, a veritable live music box, from which you may hear on one day a lively Paganini played by Adrian (reputed to be the best violinist in Bombay, next to Mehli Mehta) and on another, piano sonatas played by Ivy, Dolly or Celine, sometimes accompanying the robust tenor of Patsy. Every single member of the D'mello family had grown up with music as sustenance, and that, too, in a neigbourhood whose ears were dulled by the din of noisier engagements. Perhaps we could condone the dullness of their collective ear because the D'mellos played mainly classical and semi-classical works—a little inaccessible to ears that thrilled to the cacophony of the picnic repertoire and to big brass bands and gumats belting out East Indian wedding songs.

And then came Freddy, the youngest of the D'mellos. Kitty believed that it was his jazzy piano playing that bridged the chasm between the D'mello family's chamber music and the village's common musical denominator. He combined with Mervyn Pereira, first on the Bass Box (that ingenious double bass made out of a tea chest and catgut) and later on the drums, to present the kind of music to which the village could at least tap their feet. Kitty found herself attending all the occasions at which the Freddy-Mervyn duo was due to play. It was for her, and for the entire parish, the first taste of improvisational jazz and the syncopated rhythms of Dixieland, ragtime and bebop, far from the big-band arrangements of the Goody Seervais and Maurice Concessios of the day.

Already the grown-ups had their eye on a new wave of youngsters shoving themselves into the limelight. In Jane's Cottage on Caesar Road, six schoolboys in short pants were putting together an innocent little string band. They offered a repertoire of the day's pop—Johnny Mathis, Perry Como, Pat Boone, Cliff Richards, Connie Francis, Elvis Presley and the songs on the Binaca Hit Parade. They played with what was seen as a nice, naive bravado at school functions, the popular 'terrace shows' of those days, and other small, intimate events for which they charged twenty-five rupees, over and above which they had to be given snacks and soft drinks free. They called themselves the Rhythm Boys, an all-East Indian band, with Adolf, Jerry, Errol, Francis, Gordan and a lone skinny Mangalorean who played the mandolin. The twenty-five rupees went to build up the musical hardware needed for the band.

Music had taken over the youth scene. So dance could not be far behind. Sunday afternoons saw groups of teenagers meeting in homes with sufficiently large living rooms and a gramophone. They taught each other the foxtrot, the waltz and the cha-cha-cha, a few venturing into the jive. They were all getting ready for the next terrace show, when Amboli, Andheri and Kevni would pull together, each person contributing a hefty eight annas for the hire of lights, chairs and a few snacks. The whole night terrace show was their first taste of al fresco freedom and the unspeakable thrill of touch; of being able, with a slight, sly pressure of the guiding hand, to know the yet unknown softness behind a girl's bra; and then for some, to whisper-brag about their personal charm and daring with such-and-such girl who, when the lights were dimmed, was ready, willing but not quite able to do his bidding, leaving the less adventurous fellows feeling sissy and deprived; and of teenage lessons on how to kiss like in the movies, like Richard Burton and Elizabeth Taylor, the techniques of osculation, the lingual and labial negotiation needed for pleasure, arousal and sexual conquest. Kitty, with her passion for music and her love of dancing, attended these shows and after one of these, she would go back and smile at how neatly the little tricks of kalaripayattu came in handy when the boys' reach obeyed their libido. She could execute her defences discreetly without exposing the fellow's indiscretion.

The tremulous whispers of those boys' brags would go from ear to ear and it was not long before they reached some of those of a previous generation for whom the fist-on-face was the organ of pleasure, leaving them breathless with anger and regret at how much fun they had missed and a strong feeling that these chintoo buggars must be taught a lesson. And so, on a bright Sunday morning, on the way back from the 10-o'clock Mass, Envy as moral police gave one of our young braggarts a broken lip and a black eye in front of a whole lot of old aunties going home after the Eucharist. 'Teach you to spoil our girls, you buggar,' said our moralistic fist as he walked nonchalantly away.

Yes, change was happening. And Kitty could see it in the character of funerals in the parish.

The Principal

Father Menezes, the principal, brought his cane down, first on Kitty's right palm and then on her left. He noted, to his surprise and a little disappointment, that she did not even wince as the boys before her had done. Kitty was in Standard VII and the other two, Suleiman and Augustin, were in Standard VIII. Augustin had actually wrung his hands after each wallop and had shed tears, although Father Menezes was not quite sure if the boy was not just putting on a show to avoid further caning. They were being caned for staying out of class even after the post-recess bell had rung. He had caught them behind the school under what the students called 'the English tamarind tree', the fruit of which was neither English nor tamarind. They were throwing stones to knock down the fruit. He had occasion to taste these stolen 'tamarinds' and had come to the conclusion that the only reason the boys did what they did was because it was the only 'free' fruit tree at hand; one apparently owned by nobody and nobody having any use for the tamarinds. It also gave them aiming practice. It was a boy thing. But Kitty was often there with the boys, knocking down English tamarind for the fun of it. For a twelve-year-old girl, she had very good aim.

Kitty kept standing there after the two canings, with both her hands out, palms facing upward.

'Go,' said Father Menezes. 'What are you waiting for?'

'More, Father,' she said.

'More what?' he asked.

'You gave the boys six. You gave me only two,' she said, arms still raised.

'Go away, you silly girl,' he said laughing. But Kitty still kept standing with her arms outstretched. 'That's not fair, Father. Give me four more.' And then, after a pause, she said, 'Please, Father.'

'I don't believe this,' he said. 'You want to be caned!'

'It's good for me,' she said.

'Why?' he asked.

'Good for my hands. Makes them strong for kalaripayattu.'

'What's that?'

Kitty paused and then said slowly, 'Kalaripayattu teaches you how to be a good person. A strong person who can kill with her bare hands. But a good person who will not fight. Ask my father. He knows all about it. He is going to teach me kalaripayattu.'

The principal looked at her with a puzzled smile and said, 'Go away now, you silly girl.'

Father Menezes was not what you might call a strict disciplinarian. In an age when sparing the rod meant spoiling the brat, he made a show of carrying the cane at all times, half hidden inside the long sleeves of his cassock. He wielded it occasionally in a vain demonstration of that generally expected strictness. The school staff seemed to think that he actually chafed under the need to enforce this little thing called discipline when larger, more luminous qualities could be nurtured in children; qualities such as curiosity, pluck, adventure, creativity, leadership and social awareness. There were hushed complaints too against him regarding his alleged partiality to a certain kind of teacher, the kind that would readily step over formal strictures to be able to do something different. These latter looked upon him as a visionary, a builder of institutions; someone who had indeed raised the standard of education at St. Blaise's by bringing in a number of highly qualified and experienced teachers and putting in place new systems. His detractors, particularly among the Catholics, insinuated that his management skills overshadowed the more desirable virtues of the cloth. His immaculately shaped French beard and those carefully arranged half a dozen hairs over his balding pate gave him the image of an ecclesiastical dandy. As his starched white cassock rustled up the stairs to his first-floor office, you thought you could hear echoes of malice following behind him.

Kitty was attracted to Father Menezes and his

unconcealed sense of mischief, which she provoked every time she passed him in the corridor. She would stick out her palms and say, 'Please, Father.' And he would obligingly slide his cane down from his cassock's sleeve and give her two mock-wallops, the cane masterfully slowing down to a gentle touch on her palms; and she would say, 'Thank you, Father.' The other students were quick to observe, with a little envy, this transparently affectionate charade and it was not long before Augustine was emboldened to put forth his hand with a 'Please Father'—invitation for a hearty wallop, delivered with an impish smile behind that French beard. Another wringing of hands and a surprised 'Ouch, Father.'

At home, George and Cecilia were a little perturbed. Kitty's term report had come home with two red lines. She had failed in Moral Science and Art. When they confronted her with the matter, she shrugged it off with a perfunctory 'I found those subjects boring during this term.' Moral Science and Art were not subjects to worry about, but Kitty's parents were uncomfortable with the thought that she had failed in even one subject, whichever subject it was. Cecilia decided to speak to her class teacher, Miss Vasudha, who in turn thought fit to involve Miss Alice and the principal in the discussion. 'I'm doing this,' she explained, 'because I think we have a really bright girl here who can get first rank every time, if she puts her mind to it.' The discussion was held in the principal's office, Father Menezes being a silent participant. Kitty's reports of the past three years were put on the table. They were not bad reports by any measure: over 70 per cent in most subjects; ranking between fourth and sixth in the class. 'Why fourth? You can have the first rank every time,' Miss Vasudha repeated.

'I don't want first rank,' Kitty said. 'I hate the first rank and I hope I never get it.' A surprised Miss Vasudha looked from one person to the other in the room. She could see the hint of a smile in the principal's eyes. Alice's lips were quivering in an attempt to present an expressionless face. She looked at Kitty.

'What a silly thing to say,' she said. 'Why don't you want a first rank?'

'Look at the ones who come first, second and third,' Kitty said. 'Look at Manju and Vimla, Kirit or Lalit Kumar and Theresa. Just look at them.'

'What's wrong with them?'

'They look sad. They are not happy. They don't have fun.'

'How do you know they are not having fun?'

'They don't mix with the others,' Kitty said.

'That does not mean that they are not having fun.' Miss Vasudha sounded defensive.

'They are no good at games or singing or anything else. They won't share their notes or their pencils if any one of us has forgotten to bring ours. They just sit with their noses in their books. That is why… That is why…' Kitty left her sentence incomplete. The others in the room waited for her.

'That's why what, Kitty?' Miss Vasudha asked.

'Never mind, Miss.' Kitty looked down at her feet.

'That's why what, Kitty?' Cecilia repeated impatiently.

'That's why … nobody likes them… Not even the teachers.' Then looking directly at Miss Alice, she said, 'Isn't that right, Miss?'

Alice was caught off-guard. 'That's a very unkind thing to say, Kitty,' she said as sternly as she could.

'I'm sorry, Miss,' Kitty said promptly. But Alice, jerked into an untimely introspection right there in the principal's room, had to acknowledge to herself the twitchy truth of Kitty's observation. The first-rankers were never her favourites. Not just Kitty, the other students, including the first rankers, knew it as well. She was the darling of the naughty boys, the sporty ones, the lively ones, the athletes, singers, guitarists, stage actors and elocutionists. Not the first-rankers. She knew too that her cousin Flavia was similarly biased, as well as some of the others like Olive, Esther, Mr. Menon and, for that matter, even Father Menezes, the principal himself. Of course, they were fair in their academic evaluations, most often having to fail their favourites while they crowned the first-rankers with their gilded ranks. Favourable prejudice certainly leaned towards the other-rankers.

Kitty was a joiner; she had to be part of everything, on the sports field and on stage. Miss Flavia's pet, she was picked for the lead role in any dramatic or musical performance. And Miss Flavia was Kitty's model. Kitty had seen her do the lead role in a parish performance of *Hello Out There*. That was superb acting and Kitty had even memorized some of Flavia's tautly delivered lines. She had also heard Flavia sing at parties, everything from 'Ave Maria' to the naughty lyrics of George Formby's songs. She would like to be like Miss Flavia, actress, singer and energy capsule.

Cecilia's contention, at home and at that meeting, was that her daughter could (as she put it in Konkani) have ghee on both sides of her chapatti, to grab both rank and affection. Miss Alice felt the same, but she said that she did not consider the matter worth worrying about. 'She is doing well enough in her studies. And she is enjoying her school life. Just let her be.'

Kitty remembered how the meeting ended. Father Menezes invited her to stretch out her hands for those two dollops of the cane, for which she duly thanked him. Then turning to Cecilia, he spoke in Konkani (Menezes was another bleddy Mangalorean), 'Forget your ghee chapatti, Cecilia. I'm coming home for patrade curry one of these days.'

Alice's leaning towards talent and pluck rather than diligence and application was subtle, yet visible under the thin veneer of deference and approbation granted to the top-rankers. She smiled at the smart ones while she laughed with the lively. She clapped decorously for the class toppers on Annual Day but cheered like a teenager on the sports field. The fact was Alice loved her students; some perhaps more than the others, but love them she did. The feeling was reciprocated.

Oh, there were other teachers who basked in a similar relationship with their students. Fifty years on, Kitty was sure that all her schoolmates still re-lived the affection they shared with some of the teachers, pushing aside the sneers they reserved for a few. The village historian would in fact trace the evolution of Kevni and Amboli's refinement and culture to the influence of these teachers, particularly those who spent long years at St. Blaise's: Sir Menon, Maureen D'silva, Olive, Rita, Alice and Flavia. They taught those rough peasant tongues, which earlier tripped on the precipitous edges of a language that was not really theirs (English of the East India Company) to speak it with elegance if not sophistication; who replaced the rowdy local slang and pidgin with acceptable English; who gave Kevni, Amboli and Andheri a fighting chance in a job market that was becoming increasingly competitive; who, years on, could point to poets, journalists and professionals, many of whom had achieved celebrity status in the city, and say with some degree of pride, 'I taught that blighter.'

But somehow there was something more palpable and intimate between Alice and her students. They brought their secrets, their problems and their misadventures to her, not with any expectation of help, intervention or resolution, but with an unreasoned assurance that they could do so without fear of censure or rejection. She was the school's confessional.

Alice, it could truly be said, was having a love affair with her students. A beautiful relationship that perhaps many envied.

And then it happened. It was the last day of the academic year. The Standard X students were trooping in after lunch hour. Philomena and Reshma were the first to enter the class. Their screams brought the adjoining classes to see what had happened. On the last bench, near the window, Kirit lay slumped on the desk, his hand hanging limply by his side. A stream of blood was still flowing from a slit wrist. Alice, who was class teacher, passed out at the sight and had to be carried out into the principal's room to be revived.

Father Menezes took charge of the situation. He asked that the entire second floor be cleared of students. He first sent for Dr. D'souza and then the police. Kirit was still breathing, though his pulse was getting fainter by the minute. It must be said to the credit of Father Menezes and Dr. D'souza that they lost no time in rushing him to Nanavati Hospital.

In the panic and rush, nobody had noticed a note that had blown some distance away from the desk to the other side of the room. It was the sweeper who found it and handed it to the principal, but not before Mohan had read its contents and made it known to everyone.

In a neat hand Kirit, the class first-ranker for so many years, had written:

> There is no point in my continuing like this. Miss Alice, I cannot live without you. Every waking moment, it is you I have before my eyes. I want to kiss you on your lips and be held close to your breast. I love you so much I want to marry you. But I know that it is impossible. I know. I am too clever. I am not your favourite. I am not talented. I cannot play the guitar or run races. I even tried not coming first, but I did not succeed. I have no other way to go, but to go. I love you, Miss Alice. Kirit.

Kirit survived the suicide attempt. Father Menezes, with his many contacts in high places, persuaded the police to drop the suicide case. Kirit, of course, could not continue in St. Blaise's and was given admission into another school to prepare for the final year SSC examination. Miss Alice had to be treated for depression and was able to rejoin two years later.

Kitty had finished high school by then, but she heard that Miss Alice was never the same after that.

The reminiscence faded out as Kitty's glazed eyes looked at Hanging Gardens in his coffin. The flowers that Cliffy and she had brought were now being placed in the casket. Did Hanging Gardens ever have even a hint of romance in his life? Did he look with lust at those mini-skirted thighs and underwired bosoms? Did those trousers ever rise to stimulation? Or were those hanging pouches too heavy for arousal? With an imperceptible movement of her head, she shook off those venial thoughts.

Her own love life was in no way a journey of uninterrupted bliss but, looking back, she had no regrets and knew that she would not have had it any other way.

Byculla

BOYS TEND TO THINK THAT TOMBOYS ARE GAME. FOR anything. At least for far more than other girls are willing to allow. Eyes will rove and fingers will itch in the company of a tomboy. Well, Kitty continued to be a tomboy right through her teens, backslapping the boys, ruffling their hair and ever ready for wrist-wrestling and boxing matches. And so she found herself on frequent occasions having to administer the subtler, gentler moves of kalaripayattu to convey to the roving hands of priapic boys-growing-up-into-men that the game could go that far and no further with her. It left a lot of boys confused. They couldn't quite decode the conflicting signals of easy cheer on the one hand and prudery on the other.

'I'm a kalaripayattu-Catholic masala curry,' she would say to her college mates. 'Character and morality nicely blended into this thing called Kitty.'

The Catholic bit came from Cecilia, her mother. While still a little girl, her mother had told her that she was a miracle baby. 'You were born after eight years, and ours was a late marriage. I prayed to God and to all the saints for a baby. I was reading the life of Catherine of Siena at that time and I promised her that if we got a girl, we would name her Catherine. After your baptism, I took you and placed you below the tabernacle and vowed that I would try my best to bring you up as a good Catholic.' For Kitty, this meant listening to the lives of the saints—of Agatha, Lucy, Anastasia, Rita, of her mother's patron saint, Cecilia, of faith, hope and charity and above all, for a girl, the virtue, or rather the obligation to chastity.

All of which got pushed far back into the dusty corners of her brain when she visited her cousins in Sankli Street, Byculla. Cecilia's two younger sisters lived there, Gertie and Aileen. Gertie was married to David Jenkins, an Anglo-Indian who insisted that Byculla was the last step before London. Aileen's husband, Lambert Souza, was a Goan whose parents, according to their own account, were among the elite of Karachi before Independence and their move to Bombay.

For Kitty, Byculla was another country. They spoke another language here, which she never really got used to. It was Sankli Street English. Another accent. An Anglo-Indian slang. A fluid, changing vocabulary. A more rapid fluency. Amboli's 'bleddy' was Sankli Street's 'blahdy' and Amboli's 'baastar' acquired clipped vowels and hard consonants to give it bite and an urban sophistication.

Towards the late 1950s, as she was entering her teens, her ear picked up a word, or rather a sound she hadn't heard before, beginning with 'F' sharply delivered and whose meaning, she thought she sensed, but didn't know for sure. It communicated onomatopoeically. She was soon to associate it with an expletive, exclamation, semantic buckshot and verbal crutch.

There was a definite air of superciliousness with which these Byculla cousins looked upon Kitty, the villager, their suburbanite cousin. It helped make up for their low grades in school in comparison with Kitty's relative academic proficiency. In any case, 'the cock-eyed is king among the blind,' they said. 'We would have got first rank in your tinpot village school,' they told Kitty. Amboli and Kevni were the city's Third World countries of those days. 'You don't know nothing about nothing,' Kitty was told as she was growing into her teens.

She was about ten-eleven when she went along with Rudy, her cousin, to the Victoria Gardens to catch fish. Armed with Aunt Gertie's Sunday Mass veil and an empty Horlicks jar, they climbed down a small footbridge under which flowed a clear rivulet. In the filtered rays of the sun, it looked like a ribbon sequined with little fish, hundreds of them glimmering in the quiet flowing stream. Kitty, Horlicks jar in hand, would keep watch for that spoilsport gardener while Rudy would go down with his mother's veil and try to trap the shiny little things. That Sunday, as

Rudy bent down with his makeshift fishing net, he lost his grip and fell into the water. It was a shallow stream in which even a baby would not drown, but Rudy panicked and found himself struggling to get to his feet. He let go of the veil and splashed noisily in the water. In a moment, the gardener was seen running to the spot. Seeing him, Kitty in her best stage voice hollered, 'Save him! Save him!' Effectively re-framing mischief as accident.

Rudy was 'fished' out of the water and was teased no end after they got home. 'The only fish they caught was this one called Rudy,' became the family's new party piece. He however had the last laugh, when he showed them the Horlicks jar. There were three little black and orange fish swimming in it. They were in his trouser pocket, he told them triumphantly.

Later interactions were not so innocent. Teen talk hovered over titillating and veiled territory: the excitement of pubic exploration, the changing gender equations, cosmetics, fashion, boyfriends and girlfriends, petting, French kissing, hairstyles and pavement-bought yellow cellophane-covered pornographic literature. Social life had grown active, the two homes having become open houses for the neighbourhood youth. Young fellows wearing 'drainpipes' came calling, spending hours with her cousin sisters, while in the kitchen, the aunts agonized over what limits to set their pubescent daughters. Kitty was witness to flare-ups in both homes between her aunts and her grown-up cousins: rebellion, wet with tears, screaming concerts and unconvincing threats of leaving the house on the one side and being told to leave on the other.

Kitty met Austin at Aunt Gertie's place. She thought he was different from the drainpipes kind. About three years older, he had completed his graduation, BA in History, Philosophy and Sociology, and was preparing for his Masters'. Gaunt of face and wiry, he looked underfed until you saw him eat. He could put away a dozen of Aunt Gertie's chattambades almost unconsciously. Hair always tousled, with his shirt almost always half-tucked in, he visited less frequently than the others. He was always seen with a dog-eared paperback novel in his hip pocket. Kitty, a gluttonous reader, one day snatched it out of his pocket.

'You read Max Brand?' she asked.

'I read everything,' he said. 'Max Brand, Erle Stanley Gardner, Edgar Wallace, Agatha Christie, comics and the Reader's Digest when I'm out on the road—on buses and trains or waiting at bus stops. At home I read other stuff.'

'Like what?' she asked. Kitty had just passed her BA with English Honours. She loved literature. She had registered for a post-graduate course in journalism.

'Besides the classics, I read Kafka, Camus, Proust, Huxley,' he told her. 'In the college library I read Nietzsche, Karl Marx, Kierkegaard and maybe even some C.S. Lewis and Thomas Merton.'

Kitty was impressed but did not say so. He could be

reeling off names he had heard, just to impress. But looking at him that didn't seem likely. 'What do you want to do after your graduation?' she asked.

'I don't know,' he said pensively. 'I took those subjects because I was interested in them. Maybe they sounded big and important to me. Fiction and literature I can always pick up and read. Philosophy, sociology and history one has to study.'

'But what do you enjoy doing? What do you do ... when you have nothing else to do?' Kitty suddenly found herself conscious of showing a more than necessary interest in him.

'Well, I like to laze. To do nothing,' he said laughing. 'Which means I like to dream. Read. I like to play the guitar.'

'You play the guitar?'

'A little.'

'I play a little myself,' Kitty told him.

'Hey that's good. We must play together sometime.'

They never did. He brought his guitar along a week later, as requested, for her cousin Esme's birthday. When she heard him play, she knew that she would never play in front of him. He was brilliant. His 'Guitar Boogie' was dazzling. She had heard it played before by other guitarists considered to be good, but Austin's boogie was something else. His chord work was a string of tonal surprises, quite different from the tonic-dominant-subdominant progressions of the mushrooming guitarists of the 1950s.

He wasn't much of a singer, though. He would add a barely audible scratchy undertone to the general party noise. So Kitty found herself singing to his guitar accompaniment. Austin should play with Freddie of Amboli, she thought and wondered how she could bring them together.

On her subsequent visits to Byculla, she persuaded him to bring his guitar along. They would sit on two separate chairs across the room, she singing from those little pop songbooks that the Furtados had made popular, he improvising his own chords by ear. This discreet live stereophony (the concept had not yet caught on in Bombay) didn't last too long. The two chairs across the room were given up for the couch. They sat at the two ends of it—singer and accompanist—till songbook and daylight were consumed. In time, the distance between singer and accompanist had shrunk until strings and voice had merged into one indiscreet live monophony.

All this didn't go unnoticed in the Jenkins household. 'Do you see stars in your daughter's eyes?' Gertie asked Cecilia in a tone of glad mischief. 'Don't you hear wedding bells in the air?'

The Fonsecas

It was inclement weather in the Fonseca household.

Blaise, Dominic's father, paced up and down, while his wife Muriel fumed about the matter at hand: to think that someone from her own family would betray their trust in this way! Unthinkable. Hazel, her own daughter! After all they had done for her! Spent good money to send her to Burnley's for that expensive secretarial course. So she could get a good salary in a foreign company. Ungrateful girl. And stupid. And all that would go to some junglee Goan boy! As if there were no good boys among our East Indians! What would people say? The family would become the laughing stock of the whole village. She would have to hide her face behind her veil now when going to church. Oh! Why God punish me like this? Why? She moaned as in a funeral, the rant taking on the form of a dirge with one or another line serving as chorus and some new, inspired reproaches as fresh verses.

With long, angry strides, Muriel walked to where Hazel

was sitting, bunched up on the rexine sofa, her long hair covering her flushed face, red-eyed from weeping. In her signature pose of belligerence, hands on hip, she said, 'Tell me, stupid girl you. Why you want to marry so soon? You only nineteen years. And then why you not find a good East Indian boy?' Hazel was silent. She stifled a sob. 'Tell me, no, you stupid,' Muriel continued. 'East Indian boy no good for you, what? Tell me, no. Tell me.'

Hazel raised her head a little to look up at her mother. 'Yes,' she said softly but clearly. 'No good for me.' Shocked into a fit of temper, Muriel gave the girl a resounding slap on her cheek. Hazel didn't so much as flinch. She kept looking at her mother. 'East Indian boy. Good for you and Daddy,' she said defiantly now. 'Not good for me. I don't want to marry East Indian, Mangalorean or Goan. I want to marry Cliffy.'

Blaise stopped his angry caged walk and yelled at his daughter. 'Is how you talk to your mother, you shameless you?'

Sitting on the windowsill was Hazel's older brother, Dominic, a painful scowl on his bespectacled face. At twenty-one now, he had graduated in Economics and History. The National College, Bandra, had granted him a 50 per cent fee reduction on merit (his First Class SSC certificate had to be worth something!) and he had worked hard to secure a first class again. He passed his very first interview with the Standard Chartered Bank and was working in their Churchgate office. He had been contemplating a Master's degree or else a lateral shift to chartered accountancy. It had been a hard tug-of-war of differing wills in the beginning, his parents dissuading him from going to college. What's the use of that paper certificate? To end up as a clerk? Look at so many of our East Indian boys, clever fellows. They are doing technical apprenticeships in Metal Box, Levers or some good company and are getting a stipend too. Soon they will get good technical jobs in that company.

Dominic winced every time his parents or the elders brought up the topic of those 'alien' Catholic communities from Goa and Mangalore. He knew that his own friends felt the same as he, although there were a few who had absorbed that trickle of prejudice from their parents, but they were a minority. Youth circles were not in the least concerned about distinctions. Having attended the same schools, the new generation spoke English in more or less the same accents, using the same turns of phrase and local slang. There would be cultural differences, to be sure, within the different families, differences that the young found fascinating. They enjoyed trying out the different dishes in their friends' homes and participated in their festivals. Picnics and parties were merry jukeboxes of kunbi, koli, bhandari as well as Konkani songs. A salad bowl of cultures; what Muriel would call a bhel-puri.

Dominic made bold to butt in, partly to divert his

parents' ire from his sister. 'What's wrong with the Goans and Mangaloreans?' he asked. 'They are…' he was going to say human beings but said instead, '…Catholics like us.'

As he had intended, the room's focus shifted to Dominic. Blaise and Muriel shot a look of irritation towards him. Then, pointing to his son, Blaise said. 'It is all his fault. It was he who brought that Goan fellow into this house. You didn't find East Indian best friends, what? So many years this one Goan boy! Pretending to teach our son science and whatnot. Studying here till late night. Wasting our electricity. Chitchatting and whatnot. No place in his jhopadpatti, what? Every evening he is here. Every holiday. Playing ludo, cards and whatnot. His fault, I tell you. Dominic's fault.' Turning to his wife, he continued, 'And you, Muriel. You allowing him to eat here. Made extra hand breads and kuddi and prawn chilly fry and lonwas. Teaching son, no! See, what became of that teaching! See!'

'Now you blame me, what? And you? What you were doing then? Hajampatti or what? You were blind or what? Tell, no, Blaise. Tell.'

'Now you don't come on me like that, I'm telling you Muriel. I'm telling now. This is a mother's job: to see who-who comes home; see if daughter is making eyes quietly-quietly at who-who and all that jiggery-pokery thing. Man no see these things. Lady do.'

'You know whose fault this is?' Muriel said in a sudden burst of inspiration.

'Whose?'

'The Church.'

'What you saying?'

'That Goan Father. Father Siolkar. He culprit.'

'What you saying?'

'We had nice young-men-sodality and nice young-lady-sodality, separate-separate like always. Then he come from who-knows-where and join the two together. Like nowra-baiko, husband-wife sodality. Now you must see sodality prayer meeting. Boy-girl kneeling close-close. Bible class, boy-girl sitting close-close. Work in slum, boy-girl working close-close. How they won't make quietly-quietly eyes at each other, you tell me. Cathu was telling me many boyfriend-girlfriend became now in sodality. She seen boy-girl holding hand even, you know! Soon will say they want to make wedding.'

'So what?' Dominic countered.

'So what? Bhel-puri. That's what. Soon bhel-puri will become of our village. Goan-Mangalorean-East Indian bhel-puri. You see!'

'But that's very good,' said Dominic, now attempting a smile. 'We all like bhel-puri, no?'

'I will give you bhel-puri nicely now if you talk too much,' Blaise told him.

'And I heard something about you too,' Muriel said. 'Who is this Mangalorean Rebello girl that Cathu was telling me about?'

Dominic's expression changed suddenly. A hardening of his jaw muscles seemed to have locked the words that were in his head waiting to come out a little while earlier. He got up from his perch on the windowsill and left the room.

'What is happening with this family, I'm asking. What is happening?' said Blaise.

'What is happening to village? What is happening to St. Blaise's Church? This is our church. We East Indians paid for it for hundred-hundred years and now all these people are coming here from where all and showing off like anything,' said Muriel angrily. 'Someone must talk to bishop, I tell you.'

The Rebellos

STANNY REBELLO'S HOME IN AMBOLI VILLAGE WAS AN open house. The door of his ground-floor residence was never shut from breakfast time until midnight. Neighbours barged in at all times: housewives to borrow minor groceries or for their daily 'did-you-hear' bulletins, the children's friends to raid the meat-safe for any-time snacks, and Stanny's cronies to discuss the future of the world. Stanny was a senior journalist in the *Times of India* and wrote a column for the Sunday edition of the newspaper. This gave him the status of village oracle with the Amboliites. 'He's a smart buggar, menn. Got brains up there. Name comes in paper an' all.' His wife, Isabel, loved to cook and was known to go berserk in the bazaar every day, buying more than her family could consume. 'Ours is not just a family of five,' she offered as explanation. 'Multiply our five by five or six at least.' In those days before the refrigerator, food had to be consumed by the end of the day. So hospitality was more compulsion than graciousness. Their three children, Norbert, Shirley and Mignon, were constantly bringing their friends home at all times. So the meat-safe was always open and there was no chance of leftovers. Norbert was president of the Young Men's Sodality and would hold informal meetings with office-bearers at home. Kitty, as secretary of the Young Ladies' Sodality, was there every second day.

In that continuous eddy of friends and neighbours, Isabel had learnt the art of distance-listening and sly watchfulness. From her kitchen she knew or sensed what was happening in the other rooms; the activity, the drift of conversation, the mood and developing relationships, particularly between her children and their guests. There was mild flirtation among the friends. She saw it all but was not disturbed. What she did not want to see was anyone getting hurt, least of all her children. She knew that there were more than just fond vibes between Shirley and that Fonseca boy from Kevni. There was something happening too between Norbert and Kitty. There was more than just affection on her son's part. Of that she was reasonably sure, but she couldn't tell if Kitty felt the same about him. She was a good girl, and smart. Her lively nature could sometimes mislead the boys into thinking that her camaraderie was romance. She was free but not flirtatious. Isabel knew that under that easygoing exterior, the girl was extremely discerning. Come to think of it, the ones who should be resisting any serious alliance between the two should be herself and Stanny. There certainly was a difference in socio-economic status, which most families would be conscious of. Kitty, with all her accomplishments and charm, was a chawl girl, but if someone even made mention of something like that to Stanny, he would fly into a rage. 'One's wealth, present and future, is not in one's wallet or bank account, or even written across your forehead, as some would like to believe,' he had once told her. 'It's up there, in those folds under your think box.'

Stanny liked to think of himself as a self-made man. 'The only wealth my parents gave me,' he told his friends, 'was Isabel, my wife. They arranged the marriage and did a good job, I must say.' His parents Anton and Gladys could have set him up for life, being the biggest landowners in Kalianpur. Stanny stubbornly refused to take any money from his father when he left to come to Bombay. 'I came to this city with my two certificates—graduation and marriage. And some money in my pocket.'

Almost every paisa of that money was sunk as pugri for his first house in Jacob Circle. It was a poky little room with a small kitchen and balcony. 'That's where we made our three babies,' Isabel confided to her friends. 'In that one room. Not easy. It called for what Stanny called Control and Time Management. The Control involved sleeping in separate beds. Stanny would sleep with Norbert on a mattress in the balcony and then, when Shirley arrived she slept with me on the bed. This separate sleeping was necessary to avoid untimely arousal, what with the children around. That would make it difficult. The Time Management involved sending the children up to the terrace on Sunday mornings after Mass to "study their lessons." They had strict instructions not to come down till lunchtime. Not easy, this Time Management. Within that time you had to get into the mood and all that sort of thing, you know; all the time listening for sounds and hoping that nobody would come visiting. And then trying to accomplish things without too much creaking of beds and that sort of thing, you know. Until we heard other beds in neighbouring flats creaking as well; all the other couples too were being good time managers, you see.'

Oh yes, Isabel knew what it was to come up the hard way. Now that they had achieved some cash and status was no reason to wipe away the memory of hard times. She knew that if it came to the question of her son's marriage to Kitty or whomever else, she would not say no. But then, it was up to the two of them.

'I come here to listen to your dad, not to you,' Isabel once heard Kitty quip during one of their meetings. It could have been one of her verbal kalaripayattus but it was not. What she said was not altogether untrue. Stanny had a bagful of stories and surprising information on almost anything—from current affairs and political history to family genealogy—to which Kitty lent a rapt ear.

A frequent visitor and participant in these intellectual

discourses with Stanny was Patsy D'mello, sometimes accompanied by Nicholas Gonsalves and, on occasion, some of Stanny's writer friends. On Sundays, the group would walk home together after the 10-o'clock Mass, setting up the platform for a morning of mental stimulation made merrier by some serious elbow bending.

During one of these sessions, at which Kitty was eavesdropping from another room, Stanny shared with his East Indian friends a slice of their own parish history.

Tristao Dias Ribeiro

The narrative has to slip down a few centuries.

December 1554. Witness Tristao Dias Ribeiro down on his knees in front of the porcelain image of Mae de Deus, patron of the Ribeiro family in Lisbon, Portugal. He is weeping. Uncontrollable sobs shake his body as he kneels. His tears wet the floor. He cannot understand what is happening, nor does he try. Why these tears? Why these sobs? Why should he be crying when he is actually delirious with joy? And gratitude. He looks up at the face of the Mother of God and sobs. 'I prayed for a drink of water and you gave me wine. Oh Mother most merciful, Advocate of Sinners, Mae de Deus. My heart is bursting. I am intoxicated with thankfulness.'

He feels a soft hand on his shoulder. 'Why are you weeping, my darling?' says a voice that seems to penetrate his whole being and causes him to tremble. He looks up at the face and goes into another paroxysm of whatever it was that was afflicting him. 'Bella! Bella! Bella! It is you! It is because of you,' he says as he wraps his arms round her legs, sobbing into her long skirt, uttering her name over and over as if it were a pacifier in his mouth. He rises, still on his knees, holding on to her, sobbing. Pressing his face to her body, he raises himself slowly to his feet till his face is buried in her bosom. The sobbing stops, choked by the pillowed softness around his face. He rises still higher and his lips meet with hers, all aquiver.

'Not here, Tristao. Not in front of Mae de Deus.'

Slow, painful wrenching apart of the two lips; unwilling separation. 'Come up to our bed,' she says, more in a tone of soothing caress than seduction. 'Come my Tristao. Come.'

It's been exactly twenty-eight days since their marriage.

His return to Portugal from India was that of a national hero. He had worn his medal of honour awarded by the Portuguese Administration in India for special services rendered to the government. His father had arranged for a brass band and bouquets. The entire Ribeiro clan and their in-laws were at the port to give the hero a fitting welcome.

Before he set sail for Portugal, he had written to his parents, Francisco and Prudencia, that he intended to return to India with a bride. It would enhance his status and his allowances. All through the voyage, he spent anxious hours imagining the line-up of brides-to-be. There were eight of them to be seen, he was told. In India, he had savoured some of the native offerings and he wondered if any of the eight could match those in terms of beauty and passion. He visualized the possibilities: pug noses, pasty faces, large mouths and rag-doll figures. Never mind. He knew that when he got back to India, he could have those native offerings as standby whenever he wanted. All he needed was a wife to show off.

Bella was the first girl he saw. The moment she entered the room, it was as if he had lost his equilibrium. He couldn't believe his eyes. Could such a creature exist? Those succulent lips. Those passionate eyes. That full and heaving bosom. Her silken skin. Maddening. His head did a spin. Suddenly he couldn't see clearly. Everything became hazy. Was he on firm land? Or was he still on that rolling ship? He had to be steadied and given a glass of water. Someone helpfully even splashed a little of it on his face to bring him back to full consciousness.

He didn't want to see any more girls, of course. He asked for the wedding to be arranged quickly. He made no attempt to hide his impatience, nor could he if he wanted to. The solemn Latin rite, the much-rehearsed choir, the elaborate decorations, the lavish banquet, the many toasts to the bridal couple, the expensive wedding gifts just did not register in Tristao's consciousness. His whole being was on edge, aching for that moment when the two would be together in their room.

His family and friends had never seen anything like this before. They had witnessed the passion of couples very much in love, but nothing like this.

Tristao and Bella stayed locked inside their bridal room for three days and nights without stepping out even once for their meals. On the morning of the fourth day, they came to the dining room, quickly ate their breakfast and went back in. They stepped out again for a hasty lunch. And then dinner. To the amazement of all and the amusement of many, this went on for all of four weeks. And still Tristao walked with glazed eyes, hair all dishevelled and speaking to nobody.

One evening, before the couple could hasten back into their room, Prudencia pulled Tristao aside and said, 'Son. What's happening to you? Have you gone mad? You have a whole life before you to do whatever it is you are doing. Do you want to consume the lovemaking of a lifetime in one month? And you know what? This is not love. This is lust. It doesn't last. And then, that's the end of your marriage. Is this what you want for yourself? Is this all you have for your new bride? Lust?' Tristao just rubbed his eyes, looked blankly at his mother and went back into his room.

Prudencia was disturbed. That night in bed, she shared her concern with Francisco. 'This is lust,' she said to him. 'The flutter in the loins, not the heart. It's not right. Not good.'

'It will travel upwards,' Francisco said calmly.

'What will?'

'The flutter. From the loins to the heart.'

'How do you know?'

'I know.' He looked at her and said, 'With you it was the other way around.'

Prudencia sat up. 'What do you mean?'

'Yours travelled downwards. From heart to loin. It took a long time, though. Remember? Tristao took three years to make an appearance.'

'You're a wicked man,' she said coyly.

'With Bella it is simultaneous,' he said. 'Flutter in both places from day one. Tristao is a lucky man. We did our job well, Prudencia. Tristao has got to thank you and me.'

The fluttering continued.

Two days later Tristao and his wife were on the ship to India. The voyage was rough, crew all over the place, and so lovemaking was difficult on board. On arrival, however, Tristao made up for lost time, continuing his locked-door calendar for another week till Bella, after a particularly passionate session said, 'Tristao my dear. I would like to see what India looks like outside our house.'

It was a huge, one-storeyed mansion on a beach, much larger than most homes Bella had seen in Portugal. Outside there were rooms for the servants and service staff, a room for artillery, a large stable and a well-equipped horse carriage. Huge verandahs offered a glorious view of Versova beach. It was as if Bella owned the entire expanse because theirs was the only house on the beach. At the far end on the right she could barely see what she later came to know as the fishing village, with its strings of drying fish and fishing nets.

'All this is mine; therefore yours, Bella,' Tristao told his wife. 'And there is more. All of Versova and Amboli are in my charge; all the tax collected from these two villages is for you and me to have and spend any way we want to. Awarded to me by the Administration for all the good work I did for Portugal. Are you happy, my dear?'

'Oh, I'm so happy!' she exclaimed.

'So. Now, may we go up to our room?'

And so it was. Months of closeted bliss for Tristao, a long, unexpected holiday for the Ribeiro service staff. The carriage wheels were in danger of rusting and the tax collection needed counting and book keeping. For Bella it was an uncertain shuttling of Passion's flutter, upwards and down.

And then it happened. Bella developed a throat infection, a rather nasty form. It was as if one of those crabs she saw on the beach had crawled in and caught her by the throat. Swallowing became torture. She could hardly speak. Dr. Gaspar Baretto, a Portugese physician from Colaba, was consulted. He gave her a specially compounded mixture to be taken four times a day, which would set her right, he said. It did not. In fact, it got worse. She lost whatever little voice she had. She groaned with the pain. Yet she did not resist the calling of Tristao's urgent flutters. As a result, her husband caught the infection too. He was miserable for a week, during which time he spared her his advances. The pain in his throat was stronger than the flutter elsewhere.

But then his robust constitution got the better of that pharyngeal 'crab'. He was well again. Up and running. And so was the libidinous flutter. This time, however, Bella was firm. She didn't let him even come near her. 'No, my dearest,' she pleaded with him. 'I have this terrible thing and I don't want to give it to you again. I love you too much to do that.' This time her flutter moved decidedly upwards and lodged itself there. She stayed locked in her room for days, asking her maid to bring her cold soups from time to time, unable to swallow anything but liquids.

Tristao was in agony. His throat was fine now. But the flutter was causing his whole being to ache. He thought he would go mad. He had handled sword and musket in the skirmishes that helped Portugal acquire the lands north of Goa, suffered wounds to his body, but none like this.

The doctors seemed useless. He had to turn to others for help.

He ordered a framed picture of his family patron, Mae de Deus, to be put up in one of the many rooms. Every morning and night he went down on his knees and shed tears. 'You gave me wine,' he moaned, 'but you won't let me sip of it. O Mae de Deus, have pity on me.'

It didn't work. Tristao spoke to his confessor, the Padre Avelinho Da Cunha, an eighty-year-old Jesuit who had worked alongside that holy and amazing priest, Francisco Xavier, who had died two years ago. He told him of his devotion and prayers to Mae de Deus, which had resulted in nothing.

'It is the wages of sin, my son. Lust has its consequences. Mae de Deus will certainly not help you. I have looked at all the books and there is no patron saint of lovemaking, I assure you.'

In the locked sickroom, Bella was being visited by her confessor, Padre Armino Suares, a Franciscan. He would come every day with two candles tied into a cross. He placed the wax cross against her throat and uttered a prayer in Latin.

'What is that prayer you say, Padre?' Bella wanted to know.

'It is a prayer to St. Blaise, patron saint of those having throat ailments,' he told her. Before leaving, he painted her throat with a paste made from herbs.

'What is that?' she asked the padre.

'It is a herbal paste from a root I got in Cannanore,' he said. 'I study local medicinal plants. And then, I pray. I get guidance from above. This time from St. Blaise.'

Bella paused before she spoke. 'If I get well, I will ask my husband to build a church in honour of the saint who cured me. That is a promise I make before you, Padre.'

'And so it came to pass,' said Stanny Rebello, ending his fantastic story, 'that the Franciscans built the Church of St. Blaise in Amboli with money provided by the lusty lover, Tristao Dias Ribeiro. It wouldn't have happened if his wife had not been afflicted with a throat infection. There would be no St. Blaise's Church if not for that passionate flutter. It is a story of concupiscence and faith.'

'Fantastic story,' said Patsy. 'How much of it have you made up, Stanny?'

'Read the history books,' Stanny challenged. 'You'll find a more boring version there. And one more thing, Patsy. This puts paid to the East Indian claim on St. Blaise's Church. It was not your money that paid for it.'

'You're wrong there,' Nicholas said. 'Where did Tristao's money come from? Was it not from the taxes paid by us Amboliites?'

'You got me there!' Stanny acknowledged.

'St. Blaise amchi,' Patsy quipped jocularly.

Posco

Sunday mornings in Kevni and Amboli were what the local punster called 'time for change'. Catholic families, back from Mass, would make sure that there was enough change at home in terms of annas and pice, mostly pice to be doled out to the doorstep beggars who started their rounds after the 10-o'clock Mass. These outstretched palms were expected and welcomed because they opened a convenient channel of charity for good practising Catholics. These were all Catholic beggars, audio-visually different from the general run of mendicants in the city, whose begging bowls, designed for a cosmopolitan target, ranged from realistically painted wounds on their person to virtuoso performances on asbestos castanets, the portable harmonium (the peti) and the bulbul tarang.

The Catholic beggar worked on niche appeal. Cultural identification. The 'I Am Your Kind' stimulus. Your language. Your dress. Your church kind. Culture as begging bowl.

There was this fellow, ostensibly East Indian, dressed in a threadbare suit, necktie, socks, shoes and felt hat. The intended picture of someone who had come down in life. His begging bowl was the English Pater Noster. With measured gait, he walked up to your front steps and began with a mezzo forte, 'Aar faader warty neven hello bee dine aim…' Which, after an incoherent diminuendo, would end with a mezzo forte, 'Heymen.' If the coin touched his palm earlier, you would be spared the diminuendo. (The altar boys of the day were well-versed with the incoherent diminuendo trick, having used it for the Confiteor, which they had to recite at the foot of the altar: a loud 'Confiteor deo omnipotenti…' followed by a string of gibberish to cover up for unlearned Latin, muttered under their breath, with a clear loud 'Amen' for full stop.) Nobody knew this beggar's name. They just referred to him as Arfaader.

Then there was the woman they called Noman Morie, the Konkani Hail Mary, identifying with the Goan and Mangalorean families and still holding out her rosary for the East Indian pice.

Another Sunday mendicant was an emaciated young mother who came with a cute five-year-old boy holding onto her skirt. They nicknamed her Ave. Her begging bowl was the chorus of the hymn, 'The Bells of the Angelus'.

Ave. Ave. Ave Maria.
Ave. Ave. Ave Maria.

Some Sunday mornings would see a decently turned

out Anglo-Indian with his neatly attired son in tow. He would do a nasal microphone rendition of (how did you guess?) 'Some Sunday Morning' from *San Antonio*. Left thumb pinching one nostril and his right palm cupped over nose and mouth, he would produce an amplified, tinny, nasal voice approximating the old-time microphone sound, loud enough to be heard by at least four or five families. His phrasing was quaint, investing each word with the dynamics you generally gave to whole phrases; the loudness and intensity rising and falling from the beginning of a word to its end—a melodic sparrow hopping from one flagstone to another. He selected his homes, picking bungalows and enclosures that had more than one family. The rich ones. He got more than pice here. At least an anna from each family. He would follow his Sunday morning relevance number with songs like 'I had a home down in Texas' and 'White Cliffs of Dover.'

Nobody knew where these beggars came from. They were not parishioners of St. Blaise's. They probably came from parishes not very distant but far enough to give them the anonymity they desired.

On a hot Sunday morning, when Arfaader and Noman Morie were doing their rounds, Ave was being carried in a reusable coffin to the St. Blaise cemetery. She had been brought there by four men from the stables, the tabelas of Jogeshwari. They had found her lying on the road in front of one of their stables, with her son still holding onto her hand. They wrapped her in a dirty old bed sheet and because they had seen a rosary round her neck, they brought her to the nearest church.

It was Hanging Gardens who dug her grave and deposited her in it. The four men stood respectfully while the priest intoned the prayers. They walked away even before the grave was covered.

Hanging Gardens finished patting down the earth and as he picked up his implements and was getting ready to go, he saw the boy, Ave's little son. He was standing at a distance from the grave. Slowly the boy went and stood on the mound of earth that covered his mother. Then he sat down and started digging with his fingers. Hanging Gardens looked at him for a while. He went up to him and stood him on his feet. 'Ghar jao,' he said in Hindi, then in English 'Home. Go. Go.' The boy looked up at him expressionless. Hanging Gardens scratched his head, not knowing what to do. He began walking away, but after he had taken a few steps, he stopped and looked behind at the boy, standing there all alone, looking helpless. Hesitantly he went up to the child, took him by the hand and began walking away. As they reached the dividing wall between the higher and lower class of graves, the boy slipped out of Hanging Gardens' grasp and ran towards the grave. He stood there and in a clear, ringing voice sang:

'Ave. Ave. Ave Maria.
Ave. Ave. Ave Maria.'

Then he ran back and took hold of that calloused hand. Hanging Gardens took the boy home. He made him sit on the tin trunk.

'Bhook laga,' he said to his mother. 'Hungry. Give khaana.'

'Who is this?' Carmine asked, and then looking closely at the boy's face, she said, 'Is this not Ave's son?'

'Give khaana,' Hanging Gardens said.

'Naam kya?' Carmine asked the boy. He remained silent. Then in English, 'What's your name?'

'Bosco,' the boy told her.

'Go home,' Carmine said to him.

'No go home,' Hanging Gardens interjected with uncharacteristic force. 'Give khaana. Posco bhookha. Posco eat.'

And that's how Bosco came to live with Hanging Gardens and became his protége. The village boys called him Posco, the Konkani word for 'adopted'.

One evening, when Hanging Gardens came home, he was met by Posco at the door. The little fellow handed him a fistful of pice coins, totalling seven annas.

'Where? How? Tell,' Hanging Gardens stammered, confused.

'Come,' the boy said with a smile as he held his guardian's hand. He led him down the winding lane up to a point. He stopped and said, 'Wait. See.' Then he walked a short distance to the Pereira home. He stood by the door and sang: 'Ave. Ave. Ave Maria.'

Before he could finish the antiphon, Mrs. Pereira came out, saw the boy and smiled. She went in and came back with a coin, which she dropped into Posco's palm. He brought it to Hanging Gardens and placed it on his palm with a smile. It was a two-pice coin.

Hanging Gardens dragged the boy home and almost rudely sat him down on the trunk. Finger raised in stern admonition, he said, 'No Ave Ave. No Ave Ave. No Ave Ave.' Posco lowered his head and Hanging Gardens saw a tear fall. Then the boy looked up and said, 'No Ave Ave. No Ave Ave.'

From the next day on, Posco accompanied his guardian on his casual labour assignments—carrying wood, loading furniture and digging gardens or graves, his little fingers intelligently picking out the more delicate tasks—plucking out weeds or clearing dead leaves. He did this for a week and then one day he decided to stay back. The previous day, he happened to pass by Ignatius's garage and was fascinated by the sight of cars with their mouths and bellies wide open. He decided to have a closer look.

That day, after Hanging Gardens left for work, Posco walked to the garage. A Morris Minor was raised on bricks, its bonnet open. A young mechanic, in dirty, greasy clothes, was lying under it with a whole lot of tools by his side. Another mechanic was tinkering with something under the bonnet. Posco crept closer to the car and peered at what the bonnet mechanic was doing. His eye took in the jungle of cables, the nuts and the bolts. The rest of the world went out of focus for him. It didn't exist. That mechanical tangle was his entire world for those moments. One of the mechanics tapped him on his shoulder and said, 'Hey bachcha. Hutto. Jao.'

Posco looked with pleading eyes at the man who, of course, had no time to notice any fine feelings. Reluctantly the boy moved away, but just a little. He walked to the opposite side of the car. He bent down and looked under the chassis where the other mechanic was doing his thing. Soon he found himself lying down on the ground to get a better view of that amazing world under the car. He lay there for a long while, entranced by that black, greasy labyrinth, imagining himself running along those piped paths, trying to memorize the route taken, the turns and twists and the crossroads of that bewitching metallic topography.

It was not long before his unobtrusive presence began to go unnoticed. The garage became Posco's daily haunt. He watched every movement of mechanic and tool from his position, a little away from the car, like another child would watch a movie or a circus. He watched as parts were taken out and replaced; he watched them scrub and clean the car and then take it down from the bricked elevation. He watched as Ignatius went and sat in the seat behind the steering wheel and inserted the key in the ignition. The engine growled and then began to whirr. Suddenly there was a clickety-clack and the engine stopped. The car's mouth, its bonnet, was opened again and the mechanics peered in. They made a few adjustments. Ignatius attempted to start the car again. Again the growl, the whirr and the clickety-clack. The engine stopped. Mechanics went under the car. Others looked at the open mouth. Again the growl, the whirr, the clickety-clack. Ignatius got out of the car, put his hands on his hip and cast his eye up and down the disobedient thing and shook his head. In imitation, all the other mechanics, with hands on hip, stood looking at the car, shaking their heads, as if that would make it start.

Posco, who was watching from a little distance, came over to the Morris Minor and before anyone could stop him, he slid under it, stuck his little hand in the machinery. He groped inside the labyrinthine space for a while. A soft, barely audible 'Ave. Ave. Ave Maria' was heard coming from under the car. He extricated a small spanner that had lodged itself in the machinery and handed it to Ignatius.

It's good that men can gaze at their own stupidities and laugh, because that's what Ignatius and his men did Ignatius started the car and invited Posco for a ride in it.

'What is your name?' he asked him after the drive.

'Bosco... No... Posco,' he said.

'You must go to school,' he said.

'No school,' Posco said. 'I want to see car.'

'You must go to school,' Ignatius repeated.

Jacqui

THERE WAS NO SINGING AT HANGING GARDENS' FUNERAL.

In the new rubrics, selected texts of the last rites were read out by the priest, not sung. The singing was now left to the relatives of the diseased to initiate and lead. They did so, exercising their personal choices. You could expect the popular 'Abide With Me' and 'Lord I'm Coming Home' but every now and again, you might be struck by the originality of Grief's musical expression. Kitty will tell you of the time when this one family, silent and dry-eyed throughout an almost somnolent rite, were woken up by the song 'When they lay me six feet deep' rendered by an octogenarian with a sonorous, nasal voice, accompanied by an earnest harmonica. Another funeral was auditorium for a vibrant rendition of Bach-Gounod's 'Ave Maria' by the family soprano. Promptly the next funeral had a family singing, of all pieces, the 'Wedding Song', which ended in the words Ave Maria. Often, the undertaker's man would start a song if nobody from the family were forthcoming. Kitty tells of a funeral at which ten sons and a daughter stood silently around the grave of their mother. As the casket was halfway down, the undertaker began the song 'Mother of mine' in a truly tearful timbre. It was a 'hit' with the family and the attendees, bringing on the sniffles and the waterworks. Encouraged by this success, the undertaker thought fit to offer his 'Mother of mine' at the next family funeral, just six months later, this time that of the patriarch's.

Kitty wondered what song she would sing, if at all she did, at Hanging Gardens' burial today. 'I came back to say I'm sorry'? Or would it be 'Sixteen tons'? Either one would, in today's free-for-all ritual, be considered as liturgically appropriate as a De Profundis or a Requiem.

In the old days, before the Second Vatican Council and even for some time later, the last rites were sung in Latin by the sacristan, Jacqui. He brought his old violin along with the sprinkler to the graveside, and with muted double-stoppings accompanied his vocal rendering of De Profundis, Libera Me and Dies Irae. At these times, Kitty remembered hearing, under the firm Gregorian line sung by Jacqui, another soft, hardly discernible voice. It was that of Hanging Gardens, whose job as gravedigger was to wait till the end of the funeral. The mourners and attendees would do their dainty spade-and-mud flinging ritual, but it was he who had to finally pat the grave down with earth. To Kitty, his sung Latin, picked up by ear, sounded more articulate than his everyday speech. She also had occasion to hear him sing, again in that soft, hardly audible voice, the hymns during Mass ('Soul of my saviour', 'Maiden mother' and the like). He sang what sounded like harmony—commonly referred to as 'seconds'. If she could have turned the volume knob clockwise, she was pretty sure Hanging Gardens would have passed for a good baritone. He did not of course know the words he was singing; they were just sound shapes in his mouth, little more than vowels intercepted by phonetically approximate consonants, but the melodic line of the harmony was perfect. There was clearly a musical stave written in the man's genes.

After a funeral, Jacqui the sacristan would deposit the holy water sprinkler in the sacristy and head to his home just across the wall behind the church. He would ask Dulcine, his wife, to make him a cup of tea and then sit himself down with his manuscript books, in which the five lines of the stave sought to seduce those voluptuous notes pirouetting in his brain. For Jacqui, solfeggio was brain candy, his Jacob's Ladder to heaven, his goldmine, his holy water font. He broke down the clatter of everyday living into sembrevis, minimas, culchas, fuzas and semi-fuzas (to English ears, the musical intervals called semibreves, minims, crotchets, quavers, semi- and demi-semi quavers) assigning them the notes that turned noise into melody. Once, on a very rainy evening, when he was walking down Caesar Road, umbrella in one hand, his rebekk in another, brain busy assigning some exciting clippity-clop culchas and fuzas to a line of melody, he was rudely brought down to earth by screams of Jacqui! Look out! He leaped to the side of the road. Too late. He saw behind him a horse carriage (Amboli's hossgary) with Uncle Joe in it slip sideways on the wet road, hoss, gary, Uncle Joe and all, one of the wheels into the gutter. The driver, a little too late in seeing our dreamer in the middle of the street, had pulled the reins hard in his panic, causing horse and carriage to skid. Uncle Joe had to be helped out of the carriage, thankfully unhurt. He had a good mind to give Jacqui his signature epithet—'Bluddyfool hajaam'—for having caused the mishap, but seeing how disoriented and remorseful the man looked, he put his arm round him and said, 'Come. I'll give you a lift.' As a reward, he was treated to the first vocal rendition of Jacqui's just-hatched masterpiece.

Jacqui's initial foray into composition was not in the least ambitious; nothing like a symphony or concerto. It was the ladaain, the litany. The ladaain, in all good Goan Catholic homes, was the first item of any celebration, be it a birthday, a wedding engagement or just a get-together. It was the family's assurance that the occasion would be divinely blessed and that Advogad Saibinni, Mary, Advocate of Sinners, would intercede for mercy just in case there were any small misdemeanours on that day; for who's to tell what can happen after some jolly liquid refreshment has wet the celebratory brain. A hurriedly recited rosary would be followed by the litany of the Blessed Virgin Mary sung in Latin. It would begin with the Kyrie Eleison sequence, followed by the Miserere and then the many invocations to the Virgin Mary with the Ora Pro Nobis response.

Sancta Maria, ora pro nobis.
Sancta Dei Genitrix, ora pro nobis.
Sancta Virgo virginum, ora pro nobis.
Mater Christi, ora pro nobis…

And so it went on for another forty-five invocations. Repetition as penance—which the Goans thought to make a little easier with the introduction of song. Generally the ladaain was sung to simple tunes, almost plainchant.

Jacqui's rebekk had accompanied a number of these ladaains for which he would get a small payment. He would sing and play the same known tunes and everyone would be happy, including Jacqui himself, who saw this tradition as a natural extension of his primary function as sacristan of the parish. He saw himself as a deacon of sorts, officiating at what he considered to be the Liturgy of the Birthday or Engagement Party.

And then he got the idea of composing his own ladaains. It was prompted by something quite different from ladaains.

As would be expected, not long after he took up the post of sacristan, he was approached by a number of parents to give their children violin tuitions. He was happy to do so. He took it on as a mission: the conversion of the musical infidel to a higher, more refined sensitivity, that of the ear. Before long he had a group of ten young school boys and girls coming to his home for music lessons. He even bought violins for a couple of them whose parents could not afford them.

One of his last students was Kitty, then just eleven years old. Her mother, who had noticed that the girl had an ear for music, spoke to Jacqui and the next day bought her a half-size violin from Furtado's. He taught them to translate those dots on five lines into tones on four strings. He wrote out lessons for them, first in easy semibreves and minims before they moved on to the shorter interval of the crotchet. He began by composing easy pieces, which they played in unison. Later, he thought it would make life interesting for him if he arranged them into at least three parts.

Why not a ladaain? The thought was tempting. There was a ladaain coming up in fifteen days. Quickly he set music to the words of the litany and arranged it for three parts. Kitty remembered taking her violin to chawls in Amboli and Andheri—very much like her own chawl— and playing together with her fellow-students. They would be served boiled black chickpeas and half a banana at the party that followed. As the students' violin playing got better, Jacqui's ladaains became increasingly ambitious, his later compositions coming close to the structure of sonatinas, with distinct movements for the Kyrie, the Miserere and Ora Pro Nobis.

Kitty was one of Jacqui's favourite students, but within a few years, after she was fairly fluent in her playing, she told him that she would rather play the guitar. This was probably because she loved to sing. She had a good singing voice and the guitar would go well with her songbook.

With radio and particularly the Binaca Hit Parade making song the social lubricant of the times, bands were springing up everywhere. Kitty was soon to see a different music written on Jacqui's manuscript books. She read the titles, all lettered in as decoded by Jacqui's keen musical ear: *I love Khapri*, which on reading the music turned out to be 'The Isle of Capri' and *Lullubhai of Broadway* and other cute howlers.

Jacqui had moved on from ladaains to dance band music. He had two trumpets, a saxophone played by his brother, another saxophone played by a skinny Mangalorean mandolin player, formerly of the Rhythm Boys, who also sometimes played the banjo; an experienced drummer, Mr. Rodricks; and of course Jacqui himself on the violin. He asked Kitty if she could be his crooner and she readily agreed. It was the most versatile band you could imagine. They played at weddings, christening parties, thread ceremonies, funerals, church feasts, ladaains and even tiatrs (that fascinating form of Goan theatre).

One Sunday morning they were rehearsing outside

Jacqui's house. The beggar woman who came every Sunday and mumbled a truncated Noman Morie (Hail Mary) in exchange for a coin decided to halt her alms-seeking Ave that day in order to stand and listen to the band. Jacqui called out to Dulcine, his wife, and asked her to give Noman Morie her coin so she could go away. (Noman Morie was the name given to the beggar woman by Kevni and Amboli. Nobody knew her real name.)

'I've got my coin,' she said in Konkani. 'But I've not got my fill of music yet.'

'So you like our band?' Jacqui asked.

'Very much,' she said. Then she looked down and made as if to wipe a tear with her sari. 'Next Sunday, my nephew is getting married and there will be no music. He cannot afford a band. But never mind, never mind...' Jacqui thought he heard a sob.

He looked at the members of the band and his eyes asked a question to which everyone nodded.

'We'll play at the wedding,' he told her. 'Go tell your nephew we'll be there.'

The next Sunday, Jacqui's seven-member band, dressed in formal black and white, the men with red bow ties and Kitty wearing a red scarf took the bus to Versova. It had been a rainy day but fortunately the rain had stopped. This was an evening wedding reception. They had promised to be there by 6 p.m. They were given no formal address, just directions. 'Come to Versova, take the right turn before the

Machlimar jetty and ask for Noman Morie's house.' It was clear that Noman Morie was well known. At the right turn, Jacqui asked a group of boys playing marbles. 'Go straight down the path, turn left at the peepal tree and walk till you come to the big tamarind tree, then turn right.' The boys' directions were clear enough. But there was no road, just a narrow walking path that got slushier as they approached the peepal tree. By the time they reached the tamarind tree, their shoes were caked with mud, Kitty's high heels deciding to stick more to the earth than to her feet. From the tamarind tree, they spied the 'house', some distance away; a mud hut among many others on the far side of a swamp, identified by colourful bunting and balloons. Stones were placed at intervals to mark the path leading to the hut. They must have been mischievous stones that knew the trick of either turning over or sinking into the slush because by the time the seven, with their instruments, were able to negotiate the distance, looking like tightrope walkers attempting the high wire, their shoes, socks and a good portion of their trousers were soaked in slush.

At the entrance to the hut, Noman Morie greeted them with a smile and said, 'Don't worry about your shoes. We'll have them washed.'

Outside the hut was a strip of flattened earth, smoothened with cowdung, which connected all the huts, one to another. They were small one-room affairs that you had to bend halfway to enter. The band squeezed together on the strip in front of Noman Morie's hut. There was an overwhelming odour of 'wash'—that mixture of fermented jaggery and nausakhar or ammonium chloride to hasten the fermentation—from which illicit liquor was distilled clandestinely in these huts. Every few minutes, they saw a scrawny young fellow, shirtless and in shorts carry on his shoulders a yoke attached to two bucket-sized tins filled with water. The distillation process needed a continuous supply of water as coolant. So, you knew that somewhere in the vicinity, the local nectar was being collected, drop by precious drop in a bottle that would be sold for three rupees and eight annas.

Barefooted on that little strip in front of Noman Morie's hut, Jacqui and his band played that day. They had just had enough time to tune their instruments when they saw the bridal couple begin their march to the house from the far end of the swamp. The groom was in a dark blue three-piece suit, and the bride in a long flowing white dress and veil. Before setting forth into the swamp, they took off their shoes and handed them to the bridal train. Hand in hand, they glided towards the house with Jacqui's Mendelssohn guiding their steps, the bride totally unmindful of the fact that her milk-white gown now had, at its base, a good 12-inch border of swampy black.

Kitty crooned the popular English songs of the day to the accompaniment of Jacqui's florid band arrangements. Jacqui himself, oblivious of his surroundings, scraped with gusto his improvised variations on the violin, enjoying every moment as if he were performing in a five-star dancehall. The audience of fisherfolk and Noman Morie's Konkani-speaking relatives gloried in that exalted status that English singing lent to their gathering rather than to any real appreciation of the music itself. They sat with hands respectfully on their laps, as if in a church, while the band played Glenn Miller, Xavier Cugat and the more recent songs of the Hit Parade.

Kitty was getting ready to sing her next number, when Jacqui held up his hand and on his violin started to play the Konkani song 'Cecilia mujhe naum'. He went on to sing it, accompanying himself with double-stoppings on his violin. You could see the faces of the audience light up. When he started 'Undrea mujhea mama', some of the men got up to do a little handkerchief dance. Life had entered the party.

The scrawny young water-carrier stopped to listen to the music. Somebody called out to him, 'Peter. *Yeh re. Cantar munn.* Hey Peter, come on. Sing us a song.' Peter hesitated. He kept his yoke of tins down and as he was coming in to join the group, he looked down at his bare torso and sensed the incongruity of his being there among fully dressed people. '*Rau,*' he said. He picked up the tins and went away. A few minutes later, he returned, having put on a crumpled shirt. He had washed his face and combed his hair, but he had had no time to shave and a two- or three-day stubble showed on his gaunt cheeks. He couldn't have been more than twenty-five years old. He stood facing the band. He cleared his throat. Jacqui expected him to sing a Konkani song and was getting ready to accompany him.

'I will do this in B flat,' he said in a refined English accent. 'Just give me the key and then … I don't mind if you do not accompany me.' The banjo player gave him the B flat he wanted. Peter paused, took a deep breath and in a clear, resonant bass sang, 'Going home' from Dvorak's *New World Symphony* without any accompaniment, the rich timbre of his voice, the intense expression and his use of rubato giving his singing the depth and feeling that made accompaniment unnecessary. His solo voice was as good as a chorus. When he finished singing, there was a pause of silent exclamation before every member of Jacqui's band stood and applauded long and loud. It was a moment of shock and awe, of salutation and humility, to be given in this most unlikely of places a lesson in musical meekness. Their feeling of relative superiority had given way to one of near diffidence. Jacqui later confided that it had been a spiritual experience for him. The band requested Peter to sing some more and he did, from a repertoire that included arias, lieder and semi-classics. He sang 'Nessun Dorma', from Puccini's *Turandot*, 'Comfort ye', from the *Messiah* and some lighter pieces like 'To Celia', 'Londonderry Air', 'Santa Lucia' and others, while the band kept their instruments by; they just sat and listened. In everyone's mind there were questions relating to the incongruous relationship of voice and person. Where did a water- carrier like this learn to sing like that?

Kitty made bold to ask him that question. Peter looked long and intently at her. 'You may ask me to sing. But don't ask me questions,' he said in all seriousness. And then he added the word 'Please'.

That night, the members of Jacqui's band went home, wet shoes in hand, feeling that this was the most rewarding wedding at which they had ever played.

Kitty remembered that night now and had half a mind to begin an appropriate song to send Hanging Gardens on his final journey. If Jacqui were there, they could have sung a Gregorian requiem, but then there would be little participation. Cliffy and Hazel might join in, perhaps. She was working out the pitch in her mind when she spied Sybil, Austin's mother, now looking quite aged and not quite firm on her feet. She was hurrying to the graveside, led by Maureen, her daughter.

Austin

'Do you like him?' Cecilia asked Kitty in an attempt to sound casual.

'Do I like whom?' Kitty knew, but she asked.

'You know, Austin.'

'He's interesting.'

'Just interesting?'

'He's talented.'

'Just interesting and talented?'

'Come on Mummy. I know what you want to know.'

'So, then. Tell me, no chedua. Do you like him?'

'Okay. I like him.'

'More than the other boys?'

'I don't know if it is more. I like him in a different way, if that tells you anything.'

'Do you like any other boys in the same—different—way?'

'One or two others, I think.'

'Who, who?'

'Oh Mummy. These are things we talk about with our very close girlfriends. Not with our mothers.'

'Mother be your closest friend, Kitty. Especially in these boy-girl lafda.' Cecilia paused. 'You must get engaged. No?'

'There you go now! Like all mothers. Are you anxious to take me off your hands or what?'

'I'm anxious about people not spoiling your name. *Log kitte kitte muntat.* You know, Kitty.'

'What things you think of! And I must tell you, I don't like the idea of an engagement.'

'Why you say that, ba?'

'I think engagements are like handcuffs.'

'Men need handcuffs. Otherwise they will spoil you girls.'

'Ouch! What bad words you use! Spoil! Mummy, the best chastity belt for a girl is not an engagement ring. For me, it is the way you brought me up. Your stories of St. Cecilia, St. Rita and all the girl saints. If you have any trust in me, I don't need to be engaged. That is, if I finally decide to marry him. Or anybody else. And if you are talking about Austin, I think I can trust him.'

'You meet his parents?' Cecilia asked.

'Not yet. But he's been inviting me home to meet them.'

'I think you should, ba. They have not met you. Daddy and I have met Austin at Gertie's place. We think he's a good boy. Gives respect to elders and all. You go meet his parents.'

'I think I will one of these days.'

'You said a big word just now, chastity belt. What it means?'

'Ask Daddy,' Kitty told her mother with a mischievous smile.

Weekends were now Byculla days for Kitty. Her St. Blaise friends were not slow in putting two and two together to arrive at 'boyfriend'.

'What's he like?' they wanted to know. 'You couldn't find someone in our own parish or what?'

'Our parish boys are all so good,' said Kitty, 'that I am confused.'

'Be careful,' Shirley told her. 'Many of those Byculla boys are part of the Luniks gang. I hope your boyfriend is not.'

Kitty did meet Austin's parents, Sybil and Lawrence Menezes, that very weekend. The next day, she could report to her mother: 'You know, Mummy, lovers talk about love at first sight. It has not happened to me with a boy. It happened on Saturday with his family. What a lovely family! You can see how close-knit they are, but they don't go out of their way to show it. So well-read and talented. And musical. His mother Sybil and sister Anne have beautiful voices. The youngest, David, just ten, plays the violin like a grown-up. The father is a nice man and an appreciative audience. If I marry Austin,' she said light-heartedly, 'it will be because of his family.'

'*Kitte muntai go, chedua!* You are marrying family or boy?' Cecilia asked, laughing. 'No. I'm only making joke, gho. Family is very important. I am happy you like his family.'

George, at his morning newspaper, was amused by the conversation. 'You're all very funny. There is nothing certain about anything as yet. And you are talking about marriage. You'll soon be talking about the wedding cake and what to name the first child.'

'You fathers know nothing,' said Cecilia. 'We mothers know everything even before it happens.'

Kitty's musical courtship with Austin saw a change of venue. In Austin's home, the stereophony of their earlier sessions gave way to the surround sound of the family choir: Sybil, Anne and little David joining in the songfest. They sang from the pop songbook, the hymn book and even the Konkani repertoire.

'If you want a singing romance, let it be a duet,' Kitty's cousins teased. 'Not the Mormon Tabernacle Choir. And dammit, Kitty, singing is no substitute for serious petting.'

Kitty was quite happy with the situation, but in time she noticed that Austin was not. He was beginning to get restless and it showed. He strummed his guitar half-heartedly at first and then played the glum spectator while the others sang. Sybil and Anne were not slow in taking the hint and did the slow slink.

With all of Kitty's apparent ease and familiarity with the boys, she could certainly never be counted as a Juliet to anyone's Romeo. This tomboy was no flirt and by no means the world's greatest lover. Elizabeth Barret Browning and Emily Dickinson she had read with feeling and had enacted on her college stage the balcony scene from Shakespeare. The words were in her head alright. But on the romantic sofa, alone with Austin, they couldn't find utterance. She had read the much-thumbed Barbara Cartlands and Denise Robbins given by her Byculla cousins (though she couldn't quite see what her cousins saw in them). She had preferred the grandmother of this genre, Mrs. Henry Wood and had quite enjoyed reading *East Lynn* which she borrowed from Nicholas Gonsalves' personal library. It had engaged her for days and got her dreaming of some romance in her own life. The classic vocabulary of the romantic bower and the pop love song or the silver screen's scripted dialogue did not come easily in soft, caressing whispers from her lips. Not that there was no feeling. There was. A stirring within her breast when she sat within even arm's-length from him, a longing to reach out and touch. And more. But the words got stuck between heart and lips.

Austin was no better. His Camus and Kierkegaard were of no help, of course. He sat tongue-tied and kept fidgeting with his hands. He was more comfortable plucking the strings of his guitar than with lovers' talk. They discussed books, movies, poetry, exchanged jokes and at those moments when the feeling in their breast got stronger and more urgent, there was silence, long periods of passion without a tongue. And so the three words and of course so much more that slip out of lovers' lips so smoothly remained unspoken through the many sofa sessions they had together.

The silence turned out to be magnetic, drawing them physically closer together, to where arms reached around each other, attempting to press their two bodies into one; hands moving to caress; fingers ruffling through hair and, when assured of sufficient privacy, a hurried meeting of lips. For Kitty it was a new experience, on a plane far removed from anything she had known before. The emotions and the rush of sensations felt like a flood in which she could easily drown. And then she would stop as if coming up for air, look wonderingly up at his face and then go back to where they started.

St. Blaise's parish had one parishioner less on every weekend.

On a Sunday evening, when the rest of the family had decided to go to a movie, the sofa was as if bewitched. It exuded passions and sensations and knocked them down from a sitting position to the horizontal. Their caresses became hotter and wilder and the meeting of the lips went beyond just a meeting of the lips. In the middle of that sensual avalanche, Kitty became conscious of where this was heading. And when Austin in a near-savage gesture pulled down her skirt and reached inside for her, she sat up with a jerk and said hoarsely. 'No. Austin. No.'

'How can you stop it now?' he said breathlessly.

'I'd sooner die,' she said, getting her own breath back and smoothing down her skirt.

'Why Kitty? Why?' he pleaded.

'I don't feel right doing it. I'll hate myself for ever after that.'

'I don't understand. Don't you want to?'

'Even if I want to, I won't,' she said looking straight into his eyes.

'Come now, Kitty, please…' he said hoarsely and grabbed her with more ferocity than she thought he possessed. She pushed him hard and he fell against the centre table.

He got up and lunged at her again. 'I want you. I want you now,' he said savagely. She moved easily out of his way. 'If this is what you want,' she said as she moved swiftly towards the door, 'you better find someone else, Austin. Not me.'

'Don't go!' Austin cried, in anguished desperation. 'Please don't go. I will…'

But Kitty had already opened the door, slammed it shut and dashed out of the house as if it were on fire. There were tears streaming down her cheeks as she walked to the bus stop.

The following weeks were crammed with questions that remained unanswered for her friends in the parish. 'Hey! Where's your boyfriend? Why are you hiding him from us? What happened? Why are you here instead of there? Have you broken up?'

At home, Cecilia came straight to the point. 'Did you have a fight?'

'Not exactly,' Kitty answered as she walked out of the kitchen towards her room, not wanting to continue the conversation.

'Wait. I'm talking to you, gho,' her mother said.

'I don't want to talk about it.'

'You have to talk,' Cecilia said. 'You know that, ba. You have to talk. Today. Tomorrow. You will have to talk.'

Kitty turned back and stood at the kitchen door. There was nobody else around. 'I told you I could trust him,' she said with her head bowed down. 'I was wrong.'

'Kitty. Kitty. You cannot trust any man where this is concerned. Any man. You cannot trust. Even they cannot trust themselves.' Then she added, 'But that does not make them bad.'

'I cannot go back,' Kitty said weakly.

'Don't say you *cannot* go back,' Cecilia said. 'The question is, do you *want* to go back?' Kitty was silent, fidgeting with the buttons on her dress. Seeing her daughter's discomfort and uncertainty, Cecilia said, 'Do you love him?'

The question made Kitty all the more uncomfortable.

'I don't know,' she said. Then, after a pause, she said in a barely audible voice, 'I think so.'

'What about him? Do you think he loves you?' she asked.

'I don't know, Mummy.'

'Has he said, "I love you"?'

'No. We didn't say these things,' Kitty told her.

'I'm not surprised, ba. We are not the kind of family that says I luvyou, I luvyou—like the Anglo-Indians do—even to people we love. And I think Austin is like that too. It doesn't mean that he does not love you. It could also mean that he is not sure.'

'So, then, what should I do?' Kitty asked.

'Nothing. Wait and see what happens. It is for him to come to you on his knees. You be where you are.'

'If he doesn't come…?'

'That's the end of it. Kaabaar. Finish.' She smiled and gave one of those worn-out sayings in Konkani. '*Doriyan zaithe masli asa, ba. Dadiyare gelear, tuka easvon meltele*—there's plenty of fish in the sea, my dear. If the dadiyare escapes, you'll get kingfish.'

The dadiyare didn't run away. Kitty received a three-line letter from Austin:

I'm sorry for what happened that day.

It will never happen again.

I love you, Kitty.

–Austin

PS: I will come over to your house in Kevni on Sunday.

It would be his first visit to Kitty's house, his first visit to Kevni.

Cliffy

It was the visa that set the whole train of events hurtling towards what seemed to be an inevitable destiny, with its accompanying pain and emotional hurt. He only hoped now that all of it would not leave permanent scars.

Cliffy didn't expect the visa to some so soon. He was told that these things take time; at least four to six months. So he had applied. He needn't have done so in the first place. His Standard Chartered job was a steady one, promising to get even better. It paid well; more than most banks certainly more than those in the public sector. The figure on his pay packet had just crept past the third digit. So now Bastiao, his father, could tell the world that his son was in that illuminated four-figure circle. Cliffy had reason to be pleased with himself and with the way his bosses were treating him. The successful completion of a banking course pointed to even more elevated positions in his line of work. But, financially, he knew there were limits in India, unless you were in business. His father's tailoring venture would surely have done a quiet zoom past the four-figure gate, but then Bastiao was not one to let the world get a peep into his bank account. Or even to show it in his lifestyle. He went about kissing statues and wearing out the pews in church. He stayed put in his one-room-kitchen tenement. The Kevni chawl. His wife and he had got used to the small abode. His son would have to move into another house when he got married, and it looked like the boy was seriously in love with the Fonseca girl.

Self-employment was nowhere in Cliffy's vision. He wanted the status of a good position and right now, enough money to start a family of his own. He was in love with Hazel to the point of distraction. Of late, he noticed that he was daydreaming even at work.

The Omani visa arrived. His to-be employers, the Muscat office of Citibank, wanted him to start work within forty days. The salary offered was a mind-boggling five times more in terms of rupees than what he was drawing at Standard Chartered. With a salary like that, it would not be long before he could rent an apartment of his own. Of late, new residential colonies were being built. Some of them by the church to make decent housing affordable to Catholics of moderate means. So there was that happy possibility of his even buying a small apartment. Balking at the Muscat job now would be foolish. When he broke the news to Hazel, her whoops of joy were cut short like a badly censored movie sequence. Tears streamed down her cheeks when she realized that he would be gone soon and that they would not see each other for a year if not more.

'No,' she sobbed. 'I cannot let you go, Cliffy. What will I do?'

'I feel the same, Hazel,' he said. 'But I would be insane to miss this opportunity. It could make a difference to our whole lives.'

'But now. What do we do now, Cliffy?'

'Let's get married,' he said, just like that, from the top of his head. 'Let's do it before I leave. Then I can go to Muscat and after a while you will be able to join me.'

'Is that possible?' Hazel asked, hands clasped tight in anxious excitement.

'I am going on a fairly good position. I will be allowed to bring my wife. It shouldn't be a problem.'

The smiles slowly freeze and another mood creeps in. A dark sequence: a long, uneasy silence. Anxiety is written on both faces in lines of agony that both can read: Parents. Hazel's parents. They see, as in clear flash forward, the stubborn fury of Blaise and Muriel, the crinkled faces of wrath and prejudice, they hear the hurtful screams against community and social standing, the wounding war of words, wills and emotions. Cliffy had already been barred from entering the Fonseca home and they had to meet elsewhere: at bus stops, an occasional movie theatre, in the homes of their friends, like the Rebellos, particularly the Rebellos.

Hazel pleaded with a humility she didn't know she possessed: entreaties washed with tears, a stubborn refusal to eat for days and veiled threats of leaving the house. Verbal barbs were flung: 'Your ego is bigger than your love for your children. This is selfishness. God will punish you for it.' To her parents, appeals to reason were like fog on a warm windy day. She told them of the elevated position that Cliffy had secured in Muscat and the certainty of a very good and decent life for them. 'We won't be living in chawls, Mummy. We will have enough money to live in a good house, like this, even better,' she assured them. All of which was met with unshakeable resistance. 'Tell that Cliffy he can take his money and go buy a Goan maana,' Muriel said. 'Our East Indian girls not coming like that only cheap.' When even priestly persuasion failed (Father Siolkar's warning to them that they would be turning their backs on a sacrament fell on blocked ears), the padre advised them to have the banns announced. After the first banns, Blaise and Muriel charged furiously into the parish priest's room.

'How can you read the banns when the parents have not given their permission?'

'His parents have no objection,' the parish priest told them.

'But we have,' Blaise said.

'What is your reason?'

'We don't like it.'

'But why?'

'He is a Goan, living in that chawl. We don't want our daughter to marry like that. As parents, we have a right to decide who our daughter will marry.'

Earlier the parish priest had spoken to Father Siolkar, his maverick assistant who kept coming up with uncomfortably radical points of view on almost everything.

'Look at your parish, Father,' Siolkar had said to him. 'Count the number of old spinsters. For every married woman, you may find two spinsters or more in a family. Why? Because of stupidly strict, narrow-minded parents, who in turn were taught to be that way by a misguided clergy, intent on promoting holy orders at the expense of matrimony. Marriage, in the eyes of our church here, had to do with that soiled thing called sex, which of course was only for those who were not holy enough to be virgins. I have spoken to many of these lovely old spinsters. I have seen inside them even now, the embers of a one-time flame that was doused by nay-saying parents. Sad, Father. Very sad.'

'The church sees no reason to forbid their marriage,' the parish priest told the Fonsecas. 'If you cannot persuade them not to get married, we will go ahead with the sacrament of matrimony.'

The Fonseca home was awash with tears of entreaty on the one hand and anger on the other, but the stances did not change. Hazel told her mother that she had to get married to Cliffy and she would, come what may. 'I will leave this house if you say no to our marriage,' she threatened again.

'You can do what you want,' Blaise told his daughter. 'You are not getting married to him.'

On the Saturday after the third banns, Hazel packed a suitcase with her things, ready to leave the house.

'Where are you going?' Blaise demanded. 'That's not your suitcase. Give it back.'

'You'll get it back. Without me,' Hazel flung at him as she walked briskly out of the house.

Kitty looked across Hanging Gardens' coffin at Cliffy and Hazel and she wondered if the memory of that fateful day was as fresh in their minds as it was in hers.

The evening before their wedding day, Patsy, Nicholas Gonsalves, Edgar and Claude D'mello had got together in Stanny Rebello's home. They hurriedly put together the horseplay for a mock paani for Hazel according to the East Indian tradition. Kitty was there with some of Cliffy and Hazel's friends and, of course, the Rebellos. Kitty had brought Austin along. He came with his guitar and won the applause and approval of Amboli's music critics, Patsy and Nicholas. The Spanish guitar-slide guitar combination became an instant hit. Hazel smiled through the tears that wouldn't stop streaming down her cheeks. Dominic, risking his parents' displeasure, attended Cliffy's bachelor night.

Stanny had offered to give away the bride the next

morning at the nuptials, but Patsy insisted that it had to be an East Indian. The choice was between Nicholas and Claude D'mello. The latter was picked because Patsy thought that he looked impressive in his just-tailored suit.

Hazel spent the night with the Rebellos. The next morning, they escorted the bride to St. Blaise's. She was led to the altar by Claude D'mello looking dignified and indeed very handsome in his new suit.

Raman Raghavan

Hanging Gardens accosted Kitty with '*Jacqui gone!*'

'Gone?' Kitty was puzzled and she didn't like the look in his eyes.

'Finish,' he said. She thought she saw his jaw tremble with emotion. There were no tears, but she knew he was crying.

'What are you saying?' she asked, now in a tremble herself.

'Raman Raghavan,' he said, shaking with grief and fear.

Kitty ran, her mind in a crazy whirl, through Kevni pada's narrow lanes until she came to Jacqui's house. There was a crowd at the entrance. She knew then that she was about to confront her worst fears.

Raman Raghavan. That name was enough to send people virtually into a dementia of fear. The psychopathic serial killer was making world news. He had bludgeoned twenty-three people to death, mainly pavement dwellers in the suburbs not far from Kevni and Amboli. It was learned that a few years ago, he had killed even more people, men and women, east of the city's railway line. He killed with no motive, neither robbery nor revenge; he just brutally hit them on the head with a crowbar or a blunt object while they were sleeping. Inspector Kulkarni, who had been assigned to his case, described him as a dark-skinned, well-built man with an unkempt beard. Overnight it was as if the city had gone mad, gripped by a mindless fear. The killer struck mainly at night or the early part of the morning, but people were afraid to step out of their houses at all times. Grown children were accompanied by adults on their way to school. Ladies were afraid to walk to the bazaar for their everyday purchases without a companion. Factory workers on shifts sprinted home from their train stations or bus stops, looking out with dread for anyone with a beard. Kitty remembered her father exhorting their neighbours to be sensible. The man wouldn't dare to enter a populated village like Kevni pada, he told them. He was a coward who struck only in the dark when people were fast asleep. They were not prepared to listen to him. 'You have your kalari-whatever-it-is to fight him. You may not be frightened. We will die just looking at him.' Windows and doors, which had never before been kept closed, were bolted shut at all hours.

The very sight of a beard was enough to send panic shivers down the spines of people who seemed to have lost their reason. In a crowded slum, a man with a long beard was beaten to near death having been mistaken for Raman Raghavan. Beards became an ill-advised vanity. Dandies who had cultivated and sported their carefully trimmed chin-fuzzes thought it safe to have them shaved off. Pious homes went down on their knees and said a rosary every night to Our Lady Help of Christians to save them from the mad killer.

Kitty pushed her way through the crowd outside Jacqui's house. She looked past the doorway inside the room. Jacqui's twelve-year-old son was sitting teary-eyed on a chair while the others stood around looking mournful.

'Where is your daddy?' Kitty asked him.

'Hospital.'

'What happened?'

'I don't know,' he said. After a pause, he managed: 'Heart attack.'

'How is he now?'

'I don't know. Mummy's gone with him. And Father Siolkar.'

On checking with the people who had crowded around the house, Kitty got confusing answers.

'Raman Raghavan came…'

'He saw Raman Raghavan and got frightened,' someone said.

'It was not Raman Raghavan,' said another, 'it was a man with a beard. He was walking down the lane and someone shouted, "Raman Raghavan".'

Another more sane voice offered, 'He had been complaining of a pain in the chest for a number of days. He thought it was gas. This morning he blacked out and was rushed to the hospital.'

'Then what's this about Raman Raghavan?' Kitty wanted to know.

'A coincidence. Nothing to do with the heart attack. Someone saw someone with a beard and shouted "Raman Raghavan". A moment later Jacqui blacked out. Doctor was called. Jacqui was revived and taken to the hospital in a taxi. These people are unnecessarily making up stories,' said the sane voice.

But the stories rolled on.

Sadly, Jacqui did not make it. The myocardial infarction proved to be much too hasty and hard for a heart set on engaging the whole world in the gladder rhythms of song, dance and prayer; a heart that gave in and moved to its coda with a graceful rallentando. The shaken and sorrowing neighbours, confounded by the thorny syllables of the cardiac vocabulary, found an easier and more engaging narrative in the Raman Raghavan apocrypha.

As would be expected, the funeral procession seemed like one big mourning orchestra, musicians having come from as far as Dhobi Talao to join Jacqui's own band members. Besides the standard funeral classics, they played Jacqui's compositions. Many of his young students came with their half-size violins, trumpets, saxophones and guitars, which they brought along only as symbolic tributes to their teacher and which they did not play. Kitty walked with the band, head bowed in grief and respect for a person she considered a philosopher in his own right, a musician and a good man.

Jacqui's son Blaise and his nephew, Miguel, carried on his musical tradition with the Jacksons, a band that moved into the jazzy side of pop. Miguel took over and groomed the youth choir to a finesse that made them the most admired in the parish. He himself went on to compose, record and publish his own compositions of religious and secular songs. A consummate saxophonist, he performed with the Jazz Yatras and the international musicians that participated in those events. The Jacksons Band is still alive in Goa, led by Miguel's younger brother.

The Byculla Weekends were resumed and with them the sofa duets, not necessarily musical or even literary. Rather, a delirious ping-pong of pheromones, a rumble-tumble of emotions and mutually administered sensations that brought them to passion's brink but no further—Austin's promise of abstinence always held by a thin thread of barely human self-control.

She had to walk down the aisle to cross that line. For her there was no other way it could happen. Not in her book. She would have to speak to her mother, knowing that the earliest could be another eight months, when she would have completed her course in journalism. In the meantime, what her cousins called the Menezes Tabernacle Choir did their thing when the duet was not doing theirs. They sang harmony, tried out family recipes and swapped stories. Family visits were exchanged and the gap in comfort levels between the urban apartment and the village chawl began to slowly diminish to a level of unstated acceptance of the way things were.

The sound of wedding bells didn't seem so distant now.

The Portrait

It was during this period that Kitty noticed, among the many framed photographs that hung in the long corridor leading to the kitchen, a picture of a distinguished-looking gentleman. She was sure she had seen it before but could not remember when and where. She asked Austin if he knew who the gentleman was. 'Must be some old chap in the family,' was all he could tell her. That Sunday as she walked home from the bus stop, the picture kept coming in front of her mind like a puzzle asking to be solved. She knew that it had been a long time ago when she first saw it, a much bigger picture, but the same gentleman. As she walked home, she told herself that she would remember. She knew she had it, but it was eluding her.

She was hurrying past the narrow path between the Almeida and Pereira houses when it came to her. In a flash. She remembered. Yes. She must have been eight or at the most ten years old at that time. On passing the cave-like dwelling of Hanging Gardens, she had decided to peep in out of childish curiosity. She had seen the photograph in the near darkness of the house leaning against the wall. In that half light, the picture had taken on a three-dimensional quality and the shaded portions had merged with the darkness of the room. It was probably the incongruity of picture and surroundings that made it stick in the folds of her memory for so many years.

Yes, that was it. She had seen the picture in that house.

Before going home that night, she had a mind to go in and ask Hanging Gardens' mother about the picture. She decided against it. It was late. She remembered too that his mother had not been keeping good health of late and that the St. Vincent de Paul Society had to send the doctor on a house visit to attend to her.

The next morning, on her way to her college, Kitty stopped by Hanging Gardens' house and inquired about the photograph.

'Take it away. Why I want this big man in my small house?' Hanging Gardens' mother asked sullenly. 'He not filling my stomach. You take.'

'But who is he?' Kitty asked gently.

'He is grandfather of Anton's daddy. Anton's daddy's daddy. No use. You want you take.'

Kitty took a second, closer look at the picture. It was a bigger photograph with a larger frame than the one in the Menezes home. There was a name under the picture. Dr. Heitor Antonio Bragança Miranda.

'What was your husband's name?'

'Anton's father. Name Futusch.'

'Futusch?'

'Francis.'

On her next visit to Byculla, she asked Sybil if she knew who the distinguished gentleman was.

'He's my grand-uncle,' she told Kitty. 'Of course, I have not seen him. I don't know why he is hanging there. Actually, I don't know half the people in those family photos that you see on the wall. They have just come down from my mother's collection. We Goans like to show off our surnames and family trees. All to do with property, I suppose.'

'How grand-uncle?' Kitty wanted to know.

'My mother's mother was his sister.'

'That's not too distant.'

'Yes, but with these families, the boys' side is the important branch of that family tree. We have not had much contact with most of the family.'

'Did you know anyone called Anton or Joseph Miranda? His father's name was Francis, the Famous Photograph's grandson. Dead now. I think his wife's name is Carmine.'

Sybil's brow furrowed in thought. 'No,' she said, 'I don't think I know those people. The name Francis Miranda sounds familiar, though.'

Kitty then told Sybil about Hanging Gardens and his mother and the picture she had seen in their house. Sybil shook her head. 'I cannot see how people like that can be part of the Miranda family,' she said.

'I'm intrigued as well,' Kitty said. 'I'm sorely tempted to find out.'

'Your best bet is the family living in Goa,' Sybil said. 'In the family house in Madgaon. I believe the oldest grandson of the old man lives there. He should be pretty old himself. I think his name is Gerson.'

'Oh, but that's in Goa. I don't see myself going to Goa just to satisfy that curious cat in me.'

But that was just what she did. By accident.

It had been five years since the liberation of Goa, a territory with contradictory perceptions among both Goans and non-Goans. To many of the Goans, like Bastiao, Jacqui and others, it was like any other place in India—they could go and come as they wished. That is until 1954, when the Indian government slapped visa restrictions on travel from Goa to Indian territory. Before that it had been annual holiday country for the younger Goans born in India (and a homecoming for the older folk). They could take the steamer from Ballard Pier to Goa, a Portuguese colony, but geographically one with Karwar, Mangalore and the rest of the country. And yet it was like no other place in India.

They visitors would come back with improbable stories about mountains of mango and mackerel; of foreign goods such as Ray-Ban glasses, Parker pens, Scotch whiskeys, wines, perfumes and canned food; corned beef, condensed milk, salmon and oysters. To Indians, for whom Goa was another country, it was the curl of the nose, a sour grape given to such as these chawl dwellers. 'What good are Parker pens to tailors, cooks and bootleggers,' the likes of Blaise Fonseca would say, 'or even Scotch whiskey and fine wines to distillers of country liquor? Yes, they may buy a Ray-Ban to show off, or perhaps some perfume because they don't bathe, except on Good Friday, when they are not allowed to use perfume.'

The script changed after December 1961. Goa, Daman and Diu were open without a visa to Indians. 'Foreign is now in India, menn. We're dying of thirst here, in Morarji's Bombay. Let's go sip some Scotch in Goa, what?' And so the picnic limits for the then Bombay Catholics shot beyond the 'country'-drenched borders of Madh Island, Marve and Manori. A twenty-four-hour steamer journey would take them to Scotch and feni.

It was Bastiao Rodricks who prompted the idea. He was taking his family to Goa for the May holidays and it would be an opportunity for his non-Goan friends to come along, he said. His house in Mandrem was big enough to accommodate a family or two. Word got around. 'Coming to Goa?' people asked each other, an invitation chain in which nobody knew who the invitee was and who the host.

The very day after the start of the May holidays, three groups assembled at Ballard Pier. One led by Bastiao of

Kevni pada, the second by the Murzellos of Amboli and the third by the Carvalhos of Andheri Gauthan. A head count of twenty-seven, most of them being women and schoolchildren; only a few men. Kitty and her mother went with Bastiao's family. They were joined by Mrs. Rebello and her daughters. Stanny Rebello had to miss the jaunt because of work pressure at the office. He however had a suggestion for Kitty. 'Write a report on your visit and I will have it published,' he promised her.

'I will try,' Kitty promised in return.

'As a new province of India, with a distinct culture and identity, Goa will have much to interest readers,' Stanny told her. 'Give it your own point of view. As a graduating student of journalism, it will embellish your certificate.'

The trip was a revelation to Kitty and to the other non-Goans. What they noticed with not a little surprise was that in Goa, the Goans were a different people from those they knew in Bombay. It was like meeting a new set of people wearing the familiar faces of their friends. They were hospitable to an embarrassing extent, being able to lavish on their guests a graciousness they could never afford in the cramped quarters of the big city and which the city folk had not experienced in their city before. Clearly it was part of a culture which in Bombay would be squeezed down to the serving of half a banana and black chickpeas at their ladaains, birthdays and christenings.

And their homes! That came as a shocker to Kitty.

Bastiao Rodricks' house, with eight rooms and balconies was big enough to accommodate all twenty-seven of the holidaymakers though, of course, the three groups went their separate ways in Goa. The Murzello and Carvalho family homes were not just bigger, but aesthetically stunning, constructed in the colonial Portuguese style, with decorative pillars, covered porches and arches. Not even the 'aristocratic' families of Kevni and Amboli had houses to match the homes of the simple people of Goa. All of them had beautiful oyster-shell windows and they had wells attached to their kitchens.

Bastiao's house in Mandrem in North Goa was simpler than some of the others in design and aesthetics, his family being traditionally tillers of the soil and toddy-tappers. But it was a large house. Attractive mosaic tiles decorated the spacious living room while the rest of the rooms had neatly laid red cement flooring. Comfort was written in every corner of the house.

There were, of course, those few discomfiting moments every morning, when those live sewage systems with their gluttonous grunts and slurps would have the Bombayites squirming to protect their modesty, attempting to put the porcine sights and sounds behind them as quickly as their alimentary systems would permit. Through the rest of the day Goa was a piece of heaven.

The beguiling question in Kitty's mind was not *why* these people leave their beautiful big houses to live in spaces that are smaller than their bathrooms (the reason was obvious, the prospect of jobs and an urban livelihood), the question was *how*? How could they give up such huge physical comforts for the cramped, ungenerous lifestyle that suburban Bombay had to offer?

She travelled by local bus and took dusty rides on the occasional motorbike and even rode a borrowed bicycle to visit the homes of her Goan friends and to interview their local relations. She knew how they lived in Bombay. The Goans' homes in Andheri gauthan were at least cemented structures, many of them, cosy one-bedroom affairs with kitchen and running water. The Kevni and Amboli Goans, by and large, lived in one-room bamboo-and-mud chawls with common toilets and no running water. Kitty could not but marvel at the resilience and adaptability of a people, who in their native environment were disposed to that famed languor called susegado that comes from comfort and contentment. Their houses were all, without exception, huge villas compared to even the 'decent' houses in Kevni and Amboli, their walls a virtual portrait gallery of proud, aristocratic-looking progenitors.

In the piece that she was writing, she addressed herself to the question of whether the Goans' self-inflicted exile to a city of hardship and impoverishment was worth it at all. These were mostly people who academically had not gone beyond the premiere grau, or primary education under the Portuguese system. In Goa, they were assured of a comfortable but simple lifestyle as long as they put in their day's work in their fields, their fishing boats or up their palm trees. Some of them could hope, in time, to start a little enterprise of their own; a small provisions shop or hardware store, a bar, or for the more ambitious, a drugstore; but capital was not easy to come by. Kitty sensed that underneath that seeming contentment, there was a bubbling stream of ambition; a restlessness to do something more than what Goa offered in the way of career possibilities. The big city, particularly Bombay, presented to them a big surround screen on which they could project their vision for personal achievement. They had heard of Goans who had moved to Bombay and had risen to positions of eminence: doctors, professors, scientists, judges and even a few entrepreneurs. The city was in awe of these people who seemed to bring with them a sharper insight and another level of erudition to the city. Many of them had studied in Portugal and done some professional practice in Goa before moving to the big city. Among the not-so-educated too there were encouraging tales told of success—especially in the field of music. Bombay was the mecca of the Indian film industry and it embraced these musically gifted Goans, who could do more than just blow or scratch a tune on their instruments. They had something that even the most popular Indian music composers and directors did not possess: the ability to capture those slippery tunes in their heads and put them down into written scores for a whole orchestra to play.

This of course was not true for all musicians. Rebekkists were aplenty, but only a few could make it to the recording studio or the opera house. The others had to be happy with giving violin tuitions, playing at church feasts and funerals or taking up sacristan duties in churches, where they doubled up as assistant choirmasters.

Besides these, other Goans came in large numbers. But then, not all were professionally equipped. Many who came later brought with them no more than a functional literacy and that too primarily in Portuguese. It took them little time to realize that they had to invest in relevant skills, like tailoring and cooking. Some, particularly among the toddy-tappers, possessed that rather iffy proficiency in home distilling and were able to slip easily into the remunerative cracks of the city's prohibition, and soon acquired the corollary art of greasing the right palms for a blissful business behind closed doors.

Bombay's real estate went by an intellectual hierarchy that saw prime properties in the elitist locations of South Bombay go to doctors, judges, professors and only the top-notch musicians among the Goans, leaving the less fancy homes to be distributed according to purses and professionals that could afford them. The young fortune hunter could always walk into one of the village kudds in Dhobi Talao, where he paid a small rent till such time as he found his fortune or a bride, after which he had to look for a more permanent abode. This was not easy in that age of the pugri, euphemistically called 'earnest money'. The early birds found residences in poky apartments in the Fort area and Ballard Estate, later moving progressively northwards towards Dhobi Talao, Byculla, Mazagaon, Parel, Dadar's Salvacao Parish and then taking a huge geographical leap to distant Andheri, the focus group for Kitty's research.

Moving away from comparative lifestyles to her own philosophical conclusions, Kitty marvelled at how geography was able to transform character, at how susegado could mutate to grit, ambition and hard work in an alien environment. The chawl Goans of Kevni and Amboli went quietly but doggedly after their goals, educating their children, working on their homely enterprises and saving for a more hopeful future. On the other hand, she observed that the residents native to Kevni and Amboli, secure in the knowledge that they owned land and property, were happy just to continue in the favour bestowed on them by the British administrative system in the city. The legacy of the East India Company to East Indians was a susegado of another kind. With a few exceptions, even the fairly well-to-do and the landed gentry saw it fit to sidetrack their matriculation and hope to sit languidly in a clerk's chair in the railways, the administrative offices and municipal departments, earning enough to supplement the income from their lands and tenants. They spoke their peculiar brand of English and wore off-white drill jackets, ties and sola hats to underline their affinity to 'English' culture;

enough in their eyes to put them a few notches above their vernacular office mates.

Kitty looked across the coffin at Cliffy and his wife. The question she had asked some four decades ago in Goa seemed to have been answered there at Anton Miranda's graveside. Was all that hardship of leaving Goa and living in Amboli worth it for the Goans? The investment in hardship that Bastiao, his father, had made. Had it paid off?

Bastiao, with many like him, now lived in an apartment house, which had recently been 'redeveloped' from the former chawl into one-, two- and three-bedroom apartments. Bastiao had paid the additional amount for a two-bedroom flat. Cliffy was owner of two three-bedroom affairs in Amboli and Dhake Colony, which he had bought purely as investment and was earning a reasonable rent from them. His eldest, a son, was finishing a management degree in Australia, where he planned to settle down. His daughter was studying communications in London. And he himself would soon be migrating. This time to Australia. Another generation's adventure with the inevitable adrenaline of 'alien' environments.

Bastiao's sacrifice? Worth it, Kitty thought.

The Bragança Mirandas

'I could take you to the house of Gerson Miranda,'
Bastiao told Kitty. 'I know the place in Madgaon but I
cannot introduce you to the family. These people are big
badkaars. I'm a simple Mandrecar.'

'I could introduce myself as a journalist from Bombay,'
Kitty suggested. 'I'm doing a piece on Goa. He would be
willing to speak to me, I think.'

'Better I ask our padvigaar to give letter of introduction,'
he said. 'Padres are respected here.'

In the meeting with the parish priest, Kitty arrived at
the humbling realization that she was way down in the
linguistic and, therefore, social hierarchy of Goa's clergy.
The padre greeted her in Portuguese and when he realized
that she did not speak this, the language of respectable
people, he did a condescending sidestep to Goan Konkani.
That would be fine by him, but when that too met with
incomprehension, it was as if he had lost interest in his
'Indian' guest. The only other language he would deign

to speak was the kitchen Latin he picked up in the Pillar Seminary, but he knew that here too he would draw a blank with the girl.

He would not step down to English, that most slovenly of European languages. He spoke to Kitty via Bastiao, to whom he handed over the letter of introduction to Gerson Miranda, written in fine cursive Portuguese.

Gerson Miranda's house was a sprawling mansion built in the old Portuguese colonial design. As Kitty climbed the many steps leading up to the long and wide porch, she thought that either these people couldn't have lived till they were sixty or else they had extraordinarily strong calf muscles. But then, as she entered a small corridor leading to the main hall, she spied a couple of palanquins, which she was told were used in those 'good old days' to transport the patraos around town, whether it was to do their purchases, visit friends or to join in a religious procession. Those many steps did not need to be negotiated except by the palanquin bearers. The palanquins themselves were, in the present day, part of a home decor that unashamedly spoke of aristocracy.

Kitty gave up on counting the number of rooms as she was taken on a tour of the dancehall, the huge dining room, the mini-chapel, the many bedrooms, studies and storerooms on either side of a courtyard that divided the mansion in two. A flight of steps led down to a dark, dingy basement, where the family's slaves had their lodgings, she was told.

In the main hall, there were large frames with highly retouched photographs. One of them was the portrait of Dr. Heitor Antonio Bragança Miranda, the person she was given to understand was Hanging Gardens' great-grandfather.

She knew that what intrigued her personally was the history of the relationship between the photograph and Anton Miranda of Kevni; of how two such unlikely persons could be so closely related. And she knew that the larger story of Goan pride and their status outside Goa would fan Gerson's ego and get him to speak.

Kitty's journalism lecturers had established note taking as the pedestal on which a reporter or writer should stand her work. Kitty, however, felt she got more from an interview by just absorbing the mood of the moment; not just what was being said, but the tone of voice, gestures, expressions and even the silences. She acknowledged too that an experienced journalist would be able to do all this with pencil and notebook in hand; but she was not there yet.

Notebook and pencil in hand for the appearance of studiousness, she sat with Gerson Miranda in a large room designated as the study. Her rapt attention encouraged him to be voluble. In an accent and vocabulary that fused English with Portuguese, he waxed eloquent about the sharpness and depth of the native Goan intellect, sharpened even further by Iberian culture and miscegenation.

'Creole intelligence. "A" class in whole world,' he said. 'Professors. Doctors. Painters. Goan businessmen also are … What should I say… philosophers… explorers like Vasco da Gama. Not only profiteer like our neighbours, you Indians.' To him Goa was still Portuguese and India was another country. 'Government may change the rules but not our character,' he said with a sense of pride. He railed against the unfair labelling of Goans as susegado. 'Don't let that four-hour siesta fool you,' he said in his quaint Creole English. 'We wake up to opportunities when they arise,' he said, 'even if the opportunities are in Mozambique, Macau or Bombay. The Goan will never be poor.'

On this intellectual high ground, the Bragança Mirandas could be counted among the elite, both in land ownership and learning. Acreage, degrees and titles conferred on them by the Portuguese for meritorious work were part of their heritage.

His grandfather, Heitor, was one of them. Having completed his Setimo Ano do Liceu in Goa, he did his higher studies in Lisbon and went on to study medicine, obtained his degree with honours and won fame for his work in one of Lisbon's most prestigious medical centres. He came back to Goa to give to his native land the fruits of his learning and personal acumen.

For Kitty's benefit Gerson drew the family tree and traced the lineage of the Bragança and Miranda families back four generations, ending with the present. Kitty noticed among the last branches of the tree the names of Francis, his wife Rose (nee Fernandes) and a son named Peter. There was no mention of Carmine or Anton Miranda.

Gerson went on to talk about other distinguished members of the family, when Kitty cut him short.

'This Francis, your brother…'

'Brilliant. I would say genius. "A" class. Always first rank. Played rebekk like magician. Beethoven. Paginini. Bartok. "A" class, I tell you. Decided to go to Lisbon like our grandfather. Studied medicine. Got highest marks. Brilliant, my brother. Genius, I say. Came back to Goa to get married. His wife, Rose. Rich family. Had big house in Bombay. Colaba. Behind the Taj Mahal Hotel. After honeymoon in Macau, they moved to Bombay. He made big name. You ask anybody in Bombay. Dr. Francis Miranda. "A" class.'

'So, he was a doctor?'

'"A" class, I tell you. Evening he played rebekk. In Taj Mahal Hotel. In Bombay Chamber Orchestra. All big-big people came to his house. Doctor. Professor. Judge. Famous musician. Business people. They had many parties in his house. String quartets and all. One time Duke Ellington came. He enjoyed Goan cooking. Took cafreal masala to America. Francis was "A" class I tell you. He went to England with orchestra. Played before Queen.'

'A truly gifted person, for sure,' Kitty said in encouragement.

'But tragedy. Tragedy…' Gerson said, shaking his head.

'What happened?'

'Two years after marriage, Rose, his wife, died giving birth to their son, Peter. They tried their best to save her. And he was doctor, remember. But no use,' he said.

'That is sad. Very sad,' Kitty said. 'What about their son?'

'Peter. Francis tried his best to look after him himself. He gave up playing the violin in the evenings to spend time with his son. But it was difficult. You can imagine. But then, God is good. His good luck. He had good maidservant. Very young. Good-looking. She looked after Peter till he was six years.'

'And then?'

'We have very rich auntie in London. From mother's side. No children. She told Francis she would look after Peter for him. So Peter was sent to England. He grew up nicely. Smart. "A" class like his father. Good in studies. Good in singing. At the age of thirteen, he went to Harrow. Did good. Sang in choir. Did voice training. Sang oratorio and lieder. Very good. Francis would go every three months to see him.'

'Didn't Francis marry again?' Kitty asked.

'No. We advised him to marry. It would help to bring up Peter. But he said he would never marry again. And then, tragedy again. Big tragedy. Francis took to the bottle. Drink. Scotch. He stopped going to his clinic. He drank from morning to night. He had not recovered from his wife's death. See?'

Kitty could see that the narration was painful for Gerson. There was a long silence. He looked at Kitty and said, 'Francis died of cirrhosis of the liver.'

'What about Peter?'

'He came to Bombay for his father's funeral. He didn't go back. We heard stories of his joining the hippies. Taking drugs and moving about the streets of that terrible city. We tried to find him, but I am sorry we did not try hard enough.'

'Where is he now?'

'I don't know. He must still be in your bad city.'

The mood in the room had turned sombre. Kitty sensed that Gerson did not want to carry the conversation any further. He stood up and said, 'I think it is time for lunch.'

On the way out of the room, Kitty said, 'By the way, Mr. Miranda, do you know the name of Francis' maid?'

'What questions you ask!' he exclaimed. 'Why would I remember the name of his maid?' On reaching the table, he said, 'I think they called her Carmoo. Or something like that.'

Peter

EVERYTHING POINTED TO HER HUNCH BEING RIGHT; AND it would have fizzled out into a fuzz of teasing uncertainty if she had not doggedly gone after the slender leads that came her way.

Peter. The coincidences of name and character may not have meant anything to anybody else. But Kitty felt almost certain that the two were one person: Peter, the water-carrier with a voice, and Peter Miranda, son of Francis and Rose Miranda. She could have left it at just that, a hunch that would not have mattered to her in the least. It was not even part of her journalistic exercise on her Goan acquaintances of Bombay, but it became for her a compulsion, the skeleton of a story in her brain that needed fleshing out, a painting that needed to be finished, an itch that needed scratching. But why? The most likely motivation this narrative can offer was the link with Hanging Gardens and the portrait hanging in three Miranda homes.

Her visit to Noman Morie's house in Versova could easily have been a dead end. She was told that Peter no longer lived there. He had gone away, leaving his clothes behind. She visited the huts in that swampy neighbourhood and quizzed everyone she met there. From the 'auntie' who had employed him as water-carrier for her illicit distillation to the know-it-all children who played in the streets. Talking to a few young men, she heard that six months ago the police had picked him up from off the streets, where he had been found lying in a stupor. She visited police stations in Versova and Andheri. The latter placed her under suspicion and wanted to know what interest she had in this man, an addict. They wanted to know if, in fact, she had connections with dope peddlers and the drug mafia. It was Stanny Rebello who helped to extricate her from the thorny tangle of police procedure. Being a senior journalist, he knew the inspector in charge of the police station and through him he was able to access the file on Peter. Just Mr. Peter with no surname.

She was directed to the detox ward of the J.J. Hospital. Peter had been admitted here around four months ago, again as just Peter with no surname. He had been discharged three weeks prior to Kitty's curiosity trip. His discharge card, however, had his surname Miranda added, apparently after Peter was able to communicate coherently enough. It was confirmation for Kitty that her hunch was right. It was still a loose thread in the unfolding story of

Hanging Gardens and his mother. Nobody could tell her where Peter had gone after he had left the hospital. He just shook hands with everyone and walked out of the hospital, a ward boy told Kitty.

IMMACULATE CONCEPTION

'Don't harass me,' Carmine said to Kitty, almost in tears. 'First only all children and peoples are harassing my son Anton. Calling him Hanging Gardens and all. Now you come after me. Asking questions and whatnot and all.'

Kitty thought she had tread gently enough in approaching the subject of Anton's parentage. She had layered sympathy, praise and commendation over a single mother's achievement of having brought up a difficult child.

'I know how hard it must have been,' Kitty said with her arm round Carmine's shoulder.

'You know? What you know?' Carmine sulked. 'You are only a girl. What you know? You know nothing.'

Changing track, Kitty asked, 'Can we not get in touch with your husband's family. Should they not help you?'

Carmine buried her face in her hands and burst into tears. 'Go away,' she said. 'You don't poke your nose in my life. This is nothing of yours. Nothing of your business. You go away.'

For Kitty the answers came from a most unexpected quarter—Fiona Misquitta, widow of the late Blaise

Misquitta. After his death, she had observed a decent period of mourning, wearing black for six months, moving over to greys and shades of blue and after the anniversary Mass, slipping back into the dresses that had the menfolk drooling when first she stepped into the parish. She enrolled herself in the nearby Bhavan's College and in four years was able to put up a framed certificate of graduation. BA in English and History. 'English because I want to write and speak a different language from what they speak in my Gorai, in Kevni and Amboli,' she rationalized. 'And history because there is so much of it in the Misquitta family.'

She lent her contralto voice to the senior choir for a year or so before she decided that she was not enjoying it enough. She felt out of place, she said. 'Too senior for me,' she quipped. 'I will join them when I look in my mirror and see my first grey hair. And I promise not to dye.' She offered to sing for the Youth Sodality choir that sang at the 6.30 Mass. 'I know that you are all unmarried boys and girls,' she said at her audition. 'But then there's little difference between a young spinster and an attractive widow. Ask any of these boys.'

More than her own appearance, she brought about an almost overnight transformation in the Misquitta household. 'A family of church mice,' she was heard telling Father Siolkar. 'And it is all your fault. The Church's fault. You wanted all boys to join the priesthood and all girls to become nuns. And that's what happened in all the

Misquitta families. The boys were priests even after they were married to their poor wives. I'm telling you. They would have made love on their knees if they could. And the girls. They remained nuns throughout their lives, even though they never married.'

Father Siolkar, who couldn't agree with her more, laughed heartily and said, 'But look what you have done to them now, Fiona.'

'They go to parties. Have parties at home. We've repaired our old piano. Robert is learning the guitar. And you won't believe it, Daisy has a boyfriend.'

It was Fiona who told Kitty about Anton's mother, Carmine. 'She's a Misquittta,' Fiona told her. 'A distant cousin of Blaise. A poor cousin. That's why he built that little place for her when he saw she had no place to go. Blaise was a good fellow like that. A good man. But slightly …' she brought her finger to her temple in the well-known 'screw-loose' gesture. 'But only slightly loose. Not like the others in the Misquitta family. They were all quite "firkee", as they say in Kevni. You must have heard about Blaise's first cousin, Joseph. No? That's one firkee for you. They brought close to twenty proposals when it was time for him to get married. And the proposals kept coming because of the Misquitta wealth. He just looked at their names and rejected them. Finally when he said yes, it was to a Mary Concessio because he knew that her name matched his. What could be more blessed than Mary with Joseph, he said. A holy family.'

The couple went to church every morning and stayed the length of two Masses. For three years the parishioners witnessed these two go devoutly to holy communion every day and confession every week. Tongues did their merry wag when after the third wedding anniversary there was no sign of a pregnancy. It was rumoured that the parish priest, Joseph's confessor, had thought it fit to take him aside and instruct him in the ways of the birds and the bees and to reassure him that it was not a sin; following which Joseph was seen at the confessional every second or third day.

In a few months Mary's pregnancy started showing. Her gynaecologist confirmed that she was four months pregnant and gave her a date for her delivery: the 16th of January, the coming year. Joseph protested. By his calculation it had to be the 24th of December, most probably at midnight, because it was precisely at midnight on the 24th of March that conception had taken place, he insisted. This was weeks before the talk given to him by his confessor. He was sitting on a chair in their bedroom after finishing their third rosary to the Blessed Virgin. His wife had changed into her nightgown and was leaning against the headboard, getting ready to hit the pillow. She looked beautiful and vulnerable. He looked at her. She looked at him. Their eyes met. He remembered feeling a strong emotion accompanied by a shudder that shook his whole frame.

'Did you too feel it, Mary?' he asked.

'Yes, Joseph.' she answered feebly.

'Did you feel it down there?' he asked her, now all excited.

'Yes,' Mary answered.

'Down there in your womb?'

'I think so,' Mary said, not wanting to ask him first what the word 'womb' meant. Joseph raised his eyes heavenwards and declared: 'We are blessed Mary. You have just conceived. Immaculate conception. May it be a son.'

On the 24th of December, while everyone in Amboli and Kevni attended Midnight Mass, Joseph stood at his wife's bedside, instructing her to lie with legs apart and to concentrate on labour. 'Take a deep breath. Push. Push.' His exhortations got increasingly frantic and loud.

'But I'm getting no pains,' Mary told him.

'I know,' he said. 'You will not get the pains. You are blessed, Mary. Yours is immaculate conception. You will not get the pains. Push. Push.'

In the morning, he placed the image of the Infant Jesus in the cradle he had bought for his yet-to-be-born baby. He was sure there had been a mistake in his calculation of days. The doctors had told him that the gestation period was not exactly nine months. It was anything from 260 to 280 days. He brought out his calendar and his ten fingers to calculate more accurately.

The baby—a girl—was born on the 6th of January, ten days earlier than the date given by the gynaecologist and thirteen days later than Joseph's calculation. He gave his child the name Immaculata, firm in his conviction that it was not his embarrassing act with Mary, prompted by his confessor, that was responsible for his daughter's birth, but something sublime, something divine. The day after the baptism, it came to him that it would be perfect if the child took on his wife's maiden surname, Concessio. Immaculata Concessio would be just right, he thought. But then the whole Misquitta clan came down like hell's fury on the idea.

'What about Carmine and her son Anton?' Kitty had not lost sight of her private sleuthing.

'Oh, that was no immaculate conception for sure. That was the real thing.' Fiona giggled. 'But did you hear about the other Joe Misquitta? The Misquittas who live in the big house next to the Ferreira chawl. No? You have not heard? Well, that's another interesting firkee story. You see, the name Joseph is popular among the Misquittas. There are at least five of them in the extended family. All of them slightly...' Once again the screw-lose gesture.

'This Joe modelled himself on both the Bible Josephs: the fellow who was sold by his brothers to the Egyptians and on Jesus' earthly daddy. This Joe was a great dreamer. He believed that his dreams were gospel truth and he acted upon them.'

Kevni and Amboli still remembered that afternoon five years ago, when he went up to the belfry and began a frenetic tolling of the church bell in the manner that signalled catastrophe. As it happened, the priests of the parish had gone to the Archbishop's House for an important archdiocesan update. Joe did not stop till a huge crowd of Kevni and Amboli villagers had collected. He told them that there was a huge treasure buried behind the church belonging to the Misquitta family. It had been hidden there by his great-grandfather, Manoel Blaise Misquitta, with the help of the then parish priest, whose name he had forgotten but which could be got from the parish records. Joe was in a state of high excitement and said that it had come to his knowledge that the present parish priest had come to know of it and was planning to appropriate it for himself secretly. He had therefore arranged for three gravediggers to exhume the treasure in everyone's presence. The crowd moved over to the spot and the digging began. When the diggers were halfway through, someone thought of asking him how he knew about the treasure.

'I had a dream last night,' he said as if stating a matter of fact. 'I saw it all very clearly.' At which an irate lot shook their fists at the dreamer and walked away, angry with themselves for having responded to a madcap's call. But a group of curious parishioners hung on, expecting excitement. The digging went on for a good three hours, Joe directing them from one spot to another. When the excavations all turned out to be empty, Joe said, 'He must have already taken it and hidden it somewhere else. I must get to the bottom of it.'

Fiona paused. 'See?' she said. 'This is the family I married into. But I am not unhappy. There's never a dull moment. And all said and done, they are nice people.'

'You have not told me about Carmine and Anton,' Kitty persisted.

'Sad case. Both her parents died when she was still a girl. She spent her teenage years in an orphanage. Blaise and some of the other relatives visited her and helped in whatever way they could. Carmine was an extremely attractive girl, I was told. She later went to work in a rich Parsi house in Colaba, where she was treated as part of the family. Unfortunately the family moved to England. Carmine then started working for her last employer, Dr. Francis Miranda and his wife Rose. After Rose's untimely death, she looked after their son, who when he was six years old was sent to live with his aunt in London. Francis was totally devastated at the death of his wife. Neglected his thriving medical practice. Gave up playing the violin. Took to drink and lost all sense of propriety. It became common knowledge that he was sleeping with his maid. They were never married.

'When Francis died, she was three months pregnant. Nobody knew about it and she did not want it known. She delivered her baby in the convent that brought her up. After that she was on her own. She came to Blaise for help and he built that little place for her. They have lived here ever since. That's her story.'

That was Carmine and Anton's story. But Kitty realized that the one that preceded it, the one about Joe Misquitta's dream was significant in that it foreshadowed a later 'dream' that was to change the character and very contours of both Kevni and Amboli forever.

The Dream

About 100 metres away from Filmalaya Studio on Caesar Road is a lane on the right that was considered the dividing line between Kevni and Amboli. Until around the 1960s and early 70s it was a narrow pathway that led to a much-used well, dhobi ghat and source of water to the neighbouring hutments and swimming pool to the Amboli boys. A fork in the lane wound through a clutch of hutments, playing peekaboo behind a number of perennial haystacks. That narrow lane meandered past the D'mello bungalow right to the heart of Amboli village. The hutments that bordered the first part of the lane housed an unobtrusive group of Hindu families in a predominantly East Indian village. Some of the women were engaged in part-time 'top' work in the more well-to-do East Indian homes while others worked in the fields, helping in the sowing, harvesting and threshing of the paddy. There was, in that group, a cobbler, a plumber and a small entrepreneur who had set up a mini-provision shop that stocked the basics and small knickknacks.

The story goes that one of the younger ladies from these hutments had struck up a tender relationship with a bachelor from the East Indian home she was working in. What started with affectionate words and furtive caresses swelled into a cataract of uncontrollable passion. Their affair didn't go unnoticed. She overheard his mother tell him not to be an idiot. The woman working in the neighbouring home called her aside and said, 'Be sensible. These Christians will beat you up, and so will your husband's people. Stop this foolishness.' Knowing that it was an impossible and hopeless situation, she decided that the answer lay a few metres from her home—the well nearby. On a full-moon night, she rose from her mattress on the floor, carefully stepped across her husband, her bother-in-law and his wife and walked out into the moonlight and to the waiting well. Before she made the leap, she joined her hands and looked up at the heavenly orb and in a soft voice said, 'Chandamama, I'm coming to you. Take care of them both.'

A few seconds after the splash, the ripples that spread out like an expanding halo in the blue moonlight were disturbed by another splash, as another body dived expertly into the water. It was her husband, who had silently followed her to the well. With not much difficulty he managed to catch hold of her sari pallu, by which he was able to pull her up towards him. As he put his arm round her, she offered no resistance. Soon he had her head above water, coughing and spluttering to eject the liquid she had swallowed. Having rescued her from drowning, he had to yell for help to have her pulled out of the well. It was a deep well and he was not sure his wife would be able to negotiate the footrests all the way up.

'She lost her footing and fell,' he told the curious neighbours as she stood shivering in her wet sari.

What they were not supposed to hear was what he had whispered to her in the well itself as he lifted her head out of the water. 'I don't want you to die, my dear wife. I want you to live and be happy. You can go and marry your lover. I will not come in your way.' How was he to know that the well was a natural loudspeaker and that it was no place to whisper secrets?

She never left him. In fact, it was said later, you could not find another husband and wife more in love with each other.

So much for the romance on this side of that lane.

On the other side of the lane from the hutments, there lay a long stretch of paddy fields going right up east to the Henry Gomes Chawl; flanked on the south side by Kevni's stately houses, including those belonging to the Gomeses, D'Silvas and the D'mellos; on the north by a lush forest of mango trees, which we are told was what gave Amboli its name: Ambe Ville. Mango country extended farther north across three hills to the fringes of Oshiwara and Goregaon. Schoolboys would go picking raw mangoes right up to the first hill, while the more adventurous would climb the steeper second and third hills, which would take them through thick jungle to unfamiliar territory. There, their grandfathers told them, *their* grandfathers had hunted tigers and other wild animals. And, of course, grandfathers never lie.

But we are now overstepping the bounds of relevant geography and history.

Our piece of modern Amboli history starts around the late 1960s, when the East Indians looked around and saw that if they did not do some quick thinking, they would soon be outnumbered by those of other affinities. The housing impossibility in the city had pushed all manner of people to the luscious spaces of their village. Tristao Dias's heritage was going to be a free for all.

Their answer came in the form of the Salsette Catholic Cooperative Housing Society, a body that was formed as early as 1914 by prominent East Indians like Caesar D'mello (after whom the main traffic artery of Amboli was named) in order to protect the identity and culture of the East Indians in Bombay. It was later extended to all Catholics to give it greater legal standing. Properties registered under this Society could and can still be acquired only by Catholics. Other communities like the Parsis, the Muslims and Hindus have similar exclusive, self-embracing societies.

The expanse of fields on the eastern side of the hutments

was envisaged as the proposed Society. Committees. Conversion from Agricultural to NA. Property maps and documents. Allotments. New sales. Agreements. Arguments. Disagreements. Fights. Change of plans. Delays. More delays. It was no easy street for the Salsette Catholic Cooperative Housing Society. But on the intention they were clear and firm.

Then one morning, as the office bearers of the Society came to the site to check boundaries against maps, they were taken aback at the sight of a large group of people collected in front of the haystacks. There were a couple of policemen accompanied by what looked like a few journalists with photographers in tow, a couple of saffron-clad sadhus and a crowd of faces they had not seen before.

Stanny Rebello, who had got wind of what was about to take place, had sent word to a number of his acquaintances, including Kitty, suggesting that they be present.

'Bring your notebook along, or at least your nose for news,' he told her. 'I sense that something hugely sinister is going to take place today.'

Mr. Christie Crasto, secretary of the Salsette Catholic Cooperative Housing Society, asked one of the policemen what was happening.

'Swayambu,' was the one-word reply.

'Swayambu?' Mr. Crasto was clueless.

'Swayambu,' he repeated, and then, condescendingly, 'Shiva linga. Aatmadi hai.'

Stanny was able to enlighten Mr. Crasto. 'A swayambu is the supposititious self-sprouting of a Shiva linga, a phenomenon that calls for a place of worship at the spot. So you see?'

'Where is the Shiva linga?' Mr. Crasto asked in Marathi.

'Inside the first haystack, there,' a sadhu answered, pointing to one of the haystacks.

'How do you know it is in there?'

'That man saw it in his dream the day before yesterday,' the sadhu told him as a matter of fact, pointing again to a well-fed looking fellow in shorts.

'In a dream?' Mr. Crasto was incredulous.

'Ahaa. In a dream. They are going to look under the haystack now. You will see. Wait. '

By this time, a huge crowd had collected, most of them new faces. Pitchforks began their earnest labour, sending the hay flying in all directions as flashbulbs went off. Curious eyes were fixed on the base of the haystack while the well-fed fellow in shorts stood there looking almost disinterested, in the manner of having seen this movie before. When most of the hay was cleared, the shovels cranked to a slow motion, carefully clearing away the remaining hay, when, almost on cue, they stopped their shovelling, pointed to the centre and said, 'Bagha! Bagha! Swayambu hai. Jai Shiv Shankar. Om!'

The crowd milled closer to the spot. They saw it: a cylindrical stone rising out of the ground, rounded at the top and looking almost new. Immediately the two sadhus pushed the crowd aside and went to the stone. They had brought with them kumkum, agarbatti and sandal paste. With the latter they made three quick lines on top of the Shiva linga with a red kumkum dot in the centre, all the time intoning mantras and Sanskrit slokas:

Kumkuma chandana lepitha lingam
Pankaja haara sushobhitha lingam
Sanchitha paapa vinaashaka lingam
Tat pranamaami sadaa shiva lingam

Kitty was able to talk to one of the sadhus from whom she got some sort of translation: I bow before that Sada Shiva linga, which is smeared with saffron and sandal paste, which is decorated with lotus garlands and which wipes out all accumulated sins.

And ...

Devaganaarchitha sevitha lingam
Bhaavair bhakti bhirevacha lingam
Dinakara koti prabhakara lingam
Tat pranamaami sadaa shiva lingam

(I bow before that Sada Shiva linga which is worshipped by the multitude of Gods with genuine thoughts full of faith and devotion and whose splendour is like that of a million suns)

A small temple was erected around the swayambu, initially constructed of tin and asbestos. In time this expanded in length, height and depth with a solid concrete foundation, all of this aided by the Shiv Sena and even with donations from some East Indians, coaxed by increasingly influential political personages. Neither Kitty nor even that well-fed looking fellow in shorts whose 'dream' was being realized would have visualized the transformation of Amboli that had begun that day. Stanny Rebello, who stood a mute witness to the happenings, walked away with Kitty and in tones more sombre than she had heard coming from him before said, 'This place will not be the same again. You just watch.'

The journalist as prophet had spoken.

The Wedding

Kitty's wedding day was etched in everyone's memory in painfully hard jagged lines. If she had had her way and if it had not been for George, her father, all the photographs would have been consigned to their chula, the one coal fired stove in her house.

'The real photographs are in your head,' he told her. 'You cannot burn those away. And in any case, years from now, you may even be amused and inspired by them. You will laugh, not cry.'

The Saturday prior to the wedding, Austin had invited Kitty to a 'hop' at the Byculla Mechanics, the popular wedding and dance venue for the city's feet-happy Catholics. As it turned out, Kevni and Amboli were well represented that evening. Ten or twelve sodalists had paid their eight-rupees-per-couple that would cover heavy snacks and live music by two bands. 'Hops' had not yet evolved into the no-holding hip-shakes of later years, the hands-free swaying and gyrating which Stanny Rebello would call 'goofy sufi dancing'. The pop hops of those Byculla Mechanics events still shuffled along an intended ballroom-style, chalk-on-floor litany of stiffly formal steps. The boys would gingerly hold their partners anywhere between the cervical and the sacral regions, and their fingers would transmit tingles along their own spines in direct proportion to how new they were to holding a girl in their arms. The older, more experienced fellows would hold their partners close enough to demonstrate their expert guiding skills and execute cross steps and variations across the floor, while the learners would keep a scrupulous distance between nipples and chest and apologize every time they stepped on delicate toes.

But, as Mr Rebello once quipped, there were other foxes who would trot onto the chalk-powdered floor. They would come singly, as 'stags' and wait for the tag-and-request dances to tag or request—mostly—the girls with big breasts for a dance. What would follow was no dance; just beastly bear-hugging and worse ('your tits are hurting my ribs, I told her,' one of them was heard boasting). Their 'drainpipe' trousers would outline bulges which throbbed and thrust forward more than their feet even as their partners tried to wriggle out of their odious grasps. A virtual vertical rape in full public gaze.

It happened that Saturday. The Amboli girls were considered fair game by a handful of these foxes. The announcement of the 'request dance' became an instant net in which five of them were caught. Doreen, from Kevni, tried to discourage one of these brutes with a palm on his shoulder. When she couldn't, she pushed him with all her might. He fell and hit his head on the floor with a loud thud. He managed to get up quickly, head and ego badly hurt. He staggered right up to Doreen and gave her a resounding slap on her cheek. He had raised his hand to give her another when Austin rushed up and caught hold of his hand. 'Don't,' he said in panic. That didn't stop the fellow. He turned his attention to Austin. In a trice, one saw a brass knuckleduster in his fist.

'Luniks!' someone gasped the word. The gang was here, at least five of them.

Almost simultaneously, knuckledusters were fished out and fists flew with deadly aim and intent. Austin went down as brass met bone, his head and face streaming with blood. He lost consciousness. Larry D'mello's lip was cut and there was blood oozing out of Norbert's nostrils. It was butchery. Kitty almost went down on her knees, begging the brutes to stop, but one of them kicked in the face with his knee and went on punching the boys. It was then that Kitty grabbed a pole fixed to the ground. Using the pole as a swivel, she swung round it and her high heels knocked down two of the brutes. They went down yelping like dogs, but the other three surrounded Kitty.

'Come,' she dared them as she crouched low, her palms clasping her knees. They came at her fists ready. When they were close enough, Kitty executed a flying leap and a half-spin. As her stilettoes met two jawbones, everyone heard the sound of cracking walnuts. The boys fell in a heap and remained lying on the ground, unable to rise, cursing loudly. It was left to the last of their boys standing to help them to their feet and take them away. The rest of the crowd couldn't believe their eyes. Five of the dreaded Luniks gang laid low by one girl! That would be hard for any Lunik to live down. The story that made the rounds later (apocryphal or not, we are not sure) was that this beating was the beginning of the Luniks' end as a gang. Another version was that they weren't the Luniks in the first place. It may have been the other gang, the Fokkers.

It was a costly victory, if victory it was at all. While four of Kitty's friends were very seriously injured and sustained deep gashes, mainly on the face, Austin's condition was alarming. He had not regained consciousness. His head seemed to have been battered a number of times and was covered with blood. Someone hailed a taxi. He was rushed to the J.J. Hospital nearby. They had to rule out concussion or any form of brain damage. Kitty's right foot was swollen and she was in excruciating pain, unable to walk. An X-ray revealed an ankle fracture.

All the injured had to spend the night being treated at J.J. Hospital. Concussion was ruled out in Austin's case, but his head wounds called for stitches and, of course, heavy bandaging. Kitty's ankle was put in a plaster cast and had to use crutches.

In all the fighting and the rounds of the hospital, nobody gave a thought to the wedding-day which loomed just five days ahead. When some realist in the family finally spoke about it, Kitty suggested that it be postponed, or that it be cancelled. 'We'll have a quiet marriage ceremony in front of Father Siolkar and the angels,' she said, 'I'm not going down the aisle on crutches.'

'I'm disappointed in you, Kitty,' George said. 'I thought you would be the kind of person to walk down the aisle on crutches and stilettos even if you had not broken your leg—just to be different. Where's your spirit, your sense of fun?'

In the end, it was decided that the reception on the school terrace would be cancelled because Kitty would not be able to climb the three storeys up to it. The neighbours offered to clean up the stony quadrangle in the centre of their chawls and decorate it for the reception.

The wedding would take place.

Austin was loudly applauded as he stepped out of the wedding car in front of St. Blaise's Church and then once again as he entered the reception area. He had masterfully covered the bandages on his head with a turban to match his suit. It had been neatly tied for him by his friend Daljit Singh. Kitty let go of her crutches after Norbert, her best man, had planted a kiss upon her cheek. She floated down the aisle with both her arms around the shoulders of her bridesmaids, one on either side. Father Siolkar's homily was a rollicking parody of the Salve Regina (of the 'sweetness and the woe' of our 'poor *bandaged* children of Eve') and other inane takeoffs from the Roman Catholic Prayer Book.

One of Kitty's post-marital anxieties was that Kevni-Amboli and St. Blaise's parish would no longer be a part of her daily diary. She would now have to dodge the 'Byculla chick' tag that the rest of the city had stuck on the 'dames' of Gloria Church parish. But every Sunday without fail it was St. Blaise's 6.30 Mass for her and Austin. 'They need my alto on that choir loft,' she said by way of excuse. Brides have to be gently weaned off their mother's homes and their parishes, Austin was quick to learn, unaware of their other need to seek discreet maternal advice on matters conjugal and gynaecological.

Anyhow, this phase did not last very long. Three months from his wedding day, Austin announced that he had got his visa for a job in Muscat. He had been hired by the Sultan to teach the royal household and his close aides English, history and the social sciences, the subjects in which Austin had specialized. It was not just that the pay was good, he jumped at the invitation because he had set his mind on academics, shunning the more lucrative areas of commerce. This was academics with a difference, free from the boundaries and diplomacies of universities and conventional academia. It was like setting up his own school and university where he could design his own curricula and pedagogy.

In time, Kitty joined Citibank, Muscat, in their public relations department. It was the closest she could get to a journalistic job.

Before they left for Muscat, there was a surprise visitor to Austin's house—Gerson Miranda, who had to visit the city on business. He had good news to give Kitty and the family. It was about his nephew, Peter, who was now back in England, studying and teaching music at King's College, Cambridge. After his detoxification at the J.J. Hospital, he had to undergo a further cleansing in England, which was arranged and paid for by his rich aunt. He had decided to divide his attention and gifts equally in two directions: literature and music, with emphasis on music. Peter was doing very well indeed.

Genes are mischievous things Kitty ruminated as she gazed at Hanging Gardens' almost changeless face. Why did they have to play truant in the case of Futusch-Francis Miranda's second son, handing him a half-filled cranium and overloaded testicles, while his first-born walked away with a genetic heritage that was able to beat even the villainous designs of psychotropic substances?

The Gulf of Kevni and Amboli

WITHIN TWO WEEKS OF LANDING IN MUSCAT, KITTY FOUND herself inside the interrogation room of a police station, with the possibility of being charged and jailed for adultery. She consoled herself with the thought that the barbarous practice of stoning to death was not practised in Muscat, but sitting there, every inner fibre trembling with fear, she was not sure. They had kept Austin and Cliffy in another room, while she waited for the interrogating officer. At the door, two handsome young guards kept glancing at her as if they were eyeing some lollipop. It was a little past midnight and Kitty was afraid that she would have to spend the whole night at the police station when, to her relief and a renewal of her nervousness, the door opened to let in a small, wiry man with a beard bigger than his face. He wore a white dishdash and red, checked headgear. He eyed her from head to toe through gold-rimmed spectacles as if looking for that adulterous flaw that ought to be on her person. Finding none, he sat down behind a huge desk on a chair that could seat three of him. He squeaked a command in Arabic to the guards at the door. One of them went out and came back with an effeminate young man wearing a violet khandura. His head kept bobbing doll-like from side to side as he walked in. He bowed and gestured respectfully to the little man with the big beard. They conversed for a while in Arabic. Then turning to Kitty, the violet khandura said in a faintly British accent, 'You speak English, I suppose?'

'Yes,' Kitty said.

'OK, then I am your interpreter. You have been arrested on a charge of adultery. You were caught in a compromising situation with a man who is not your husband, late at night in a dark corner. Adultery is a serious offence and you may be flogged, jailed or deported depending on what you say and on the evidence given by the police. Do you understand what I say?'

'Yes,' Kitty said. 'But I was not doing anything adulterous. It was just a game.'

There was again an exchange in Arabic between the two men. The interrogator looked sternly at Kitty.

'The respected officer says that adultery is not a good game to play. Not here in Oman.'

Kitty could not quite fathom whether she was dealing with incomprehension, cussedness or just mischief. She was beginning to despair of communicating with these people, knowing that her interpreter could do anything from silly transliteration to malevolent distortion. And then, her story, as she was trying to craft the narrative in her head, bordered on the ridiculous. It would be laughed at, and the laughter translated into whiplashes in her imagination.

It was a crazy, unlikely story. The whole fiasco was a result of their exuberance and happiness with regard to the city they were now going to live in.

When Austin and Kitty arrived in Muscat, they came expecting an alien and hostile social milieu. They were in for some happy surprises. Their first Sunday Mass was a shocker. They met more friends and acquaintances there than they did back home in Mumbai. In time, they did more than meet; they invited each other over, even more than they did in their already open-door homes in Kevni and Amboli.

When Cliffy and Hazel heard that their friends were in Muscat, they decided to come over from Dubai for a weekend visit. That called for some celebration. Austin and Kitty invited some more friends over for dinner, which turned out to be a rollicking session of well-lubricated dance and song that included, for good measure, the rowdy rhythms of the East Indian and Konkani repertoire.

Dinner done, Kitty realized that she had forgotten the dessert. So they all trooped down to the nearby ice-cream parlour. Kitty was the last to leave the house, since she had to make sure the door was locked. Cliffy stayed behind to keep her company. They were trailing behind the others when Kitty heard Austin say with some anxiousness, 'Hey, where is Kitty?' In an impish moment, she caught Cliffy by the hand and pulled him into a corner. 'Hide,' she whispered, 'let's have some fun.' They giggled as the rest of the group kept looking for them. It was a good game of adult peekaboo. That's what they thought until they heard a gruff voice say something in Arabic. A bright torchlight was shone in their faces. They were blinded for a moment but soon realized that they were facing a grey-uniformed policeman.

He looked at Cliffy and pointing to Kitty he growled, 'Who?'

With a smile, Cliffy said, 'She's my friend.'

'Friend? Not wife?' he asked.

'Not wife. Friend,' Cliffy told him.

Immediately the policeman whipped out a pair of manacles and had the two offenders handcuffed and driven away in a police vehicle. By that time, the rest of the Mumbai party had arrived at the scene of the arrest and Austin had tried to intercept and explain the situation to the policeman, but between English and Arabic, between police law and nervous incoherence, explanations had not a chance of being heard.

At the police station, both Kitty and Cliffy in their respective rooms found themselves giving up hope of explaining their way out of the thorny tangle in which they had got themselves.

It was around two in the morning. Austin was sitting in the waiting room, head buried in his lap, a classic rendering of the weeping prophet. He rose in cinematic slow motion, propelled it would seem by some dream, and almost sleepwalked to the officer on duty. From his pocket he fished out his wallet and began rummaging through it when the officer barked at him in English: 'What do you think you are doing? This is not India. We don't take bribes here!'

'But Sir,' Austin protested with a smile, 'I am not trying to bribe you. I was only looking for my identity card and my pass to the Sultan's palace.'

'What's that you said?' the man asked.

'My pass to the Sultan's palace. I seem to have misplaced it... Ah! Here it is.' He took it out and showed it to the officer together with his identity card.

'How did you get this?'

'I am the palace professor. I teach the Sultan's family English and other subjects.'

The officer paused. He looked at Austin as if to size him up.

'Let me have that pass,' he said, 'I will give it back to you in a minute.'

'I cannot do that,' Austin said, 'I have been warned not to part with it.'

'But we are the police,' the officer said.

Austin thought about it for a while before handing it over.

'I want it back,' he said sternly, raising a finger of admonition.

The officer took it with him and was gone for a good fifteen minutes. He came back with the pass and handed it back to Austin.

'There's been a misunderstanding,' he said with a weak smile as emollient. 'Your wife and the gentleman were brought here because they seemed to have lost their way and the police were only trying to help them. Now that you are here, we can release them and they can go with you. That's what the police records say. No problem now.'

They left the police station with glad khuda hafeezes and much waving of hands.

Back home, breakfast took on a celebratory tone with jocular banter and superlative testimonials to the police state of Oman. It marked the renewal of their favourable feeling towards Muscat and an affirmation of the rightness of their decision to make the move. They knew they were part of an exodus and had often caught themselves suppressing their feelings of being part of a herd.

'The Gulf' had become the promised land for many; land flowing with jobs, black gold and money. At a time when jobs were not easy to come by even in cities like Mumbai and with pay packets refusing to stretch across a month's groceries, salvation for what was the middle class then was a two-hour plane ride away. Airline routes all embraced the commercial hubs of the Middle East despite the anguished cabin crew bemoaning the toilet training of adult Indians. Full flights took off every day from Mumbai and Trivandrum to Dubai, Sharjah, Muscat and the cities of the UAE. On their way back on leave from their jobs, they were seen, mainly Malayalees and Catholics, trying to squeeze through the green channel—the Malayalees with boom boxes and TV sets wrapped in coloured plastic mats, and the Catholics with chocolates, canned food, cheeses and gaudy synthetic silks, haggling with Indian customs officials about how much grease would be needed for palms to get sufficiently slippery to let them through.

Kevni and Amboli seemed intent on emptying their talent pool into the 'Gulf' as they called it. The first to go were the lower, then the middle-level technicians and those whose qualifications and experience seemed unsaleable in the ruthlessly competitive job environment in India. Soon there were calls for senior executives, scientists, engineers, journalists and communication professionals for the many new companies and agencies being set up in Dubai, Abu Dhabi, Muscat and elsewhere in the UAE. Brown-skinned acumen soon proved a better buy than their paler counterparts from further west.

Except for St. Blaise's Church, Caesar Road and the geography on either side of it, Kevni, Amboli and Andheri were virtually transported to the Middle East along with their native cuisine, song and vocabulary. Get-togethers happened with a snap of dinar-and-rial-warmed fingers and ready cash bought them a level of entertaining elegance they had never known back home. Scotch whiskey replaced the home-made 'aunties' brew and the recent IMFLs (Indian Made Foreign Liquors). Pistachios, exotic nuts and gourmet cheeses—Camembert, Roquefort and Brie—nudged out sev chivda, ghatia and roasted papad as cocktail accompaniments. Party conversation too swung gladly away from those cranky chants about how hard life was for women to exciting information about department stores and gold souks; the men just went along| with the flow of Scotch and soda.

This was Kevni-Amboli relocated and given a shine.

The old Kevni-Amboli divide vanished as friends became closer than relations. There was Norbert D'mello from Amboli and his wife Celeste, Ronnie from Citibank, Mark Gomes and Marina from Kevni with Trevor D'souza, also of Kevni, who joined around the same time—Mario Crasto of Amboli joined much later. All PDO (Petrol Development of Oman) people. Before she could finish a finger count of her village compatriots, Kitty had a notebook full of telephone numbers, not just of St. Blaise's parishioners but of friends from across Mumbai, Goa and Bangalore, all potential invitees to her home.

They kept coming as if by some Star Wars teleportation, first the men, then their wives. The babies came soon enough. The earlier ones were delivered at home in India and then brought to live in the UAE, with grandmothers in tow as babysitters. Later, as confidence in the medical profession grew, Indian babies greeted the UAE with their first awesome birthing cries.

Austin and Kitty saw Mario and Trevor babysit Mark's babies as they came. When Mario and Trevor had their own, they got their parents to do it at first, but that could not last long. Friends ran babysitting relays and enjoyed every moment of it.

Kevni, Amboli and Andheri coalesced into one family in the Middle East. What would have been social gatherings back home became family affairs here. A whole new generation of Kevni-Amboliites was snatched away from the bosom of the twin villages, not just temporarily, but as it turned out in many cases, forever. The 'enGulfed' children grew up and studied in the international schools set up in the Middle East and later pursued higher studies in British, American and Australian universities.

Kevni-Amboli-Andheri was witnessing a transmigration of souls, a gradual emptying of character, of spirit and the very essence of life as it existed just a few years earlier.

'Our village is dying,' the old men, the paithyoos, would moan. 'Our children are going away and bhel-puri is coming now. What to do?'

Home on holiday, the 'Gulfees' would get together over duty-free spirits, exchange notes, and share their personal plans for the future. They had tasted the good life and they could not settle for less now, despite the strong tug of nostalgia and sentiment.

'The Gulf-run-fun will soon end,' Robin said, mouthing truism as if it were prophecy, 'and we will have to vamoose. Make as much as you can and then run.'

'Run to where?' asked the others

'I'm coming back home, baba,' Bertram said. 'Property and all that, you know. Otherwise jamela will become.' Back in Amboli even the 'foreign-returned' had to come back home to local vocabulary.

'Forget it,' said Robin. 'I'm not coming back to the garbage—both literal and metaphorical.'

Bertram: 'What means that?'

'Garbage. Man! Garbage. All that stink along the roads, those overflowing dustbins; all that money you have to spill under the table if you want anything from a ration card to your house papers signed; the putrid politics of caste, class and communalism; the inefficiency of the Congress, the bigotry of the BJP, the Shiv Sena and the many Sanghs. Garbage. Kuchchra. I am not going to spend the rest of my life with all that.'

'So, where will you go?'

'Where everyone else like me is planning to go. To Canada, to Australia. To New Zealand. To honest places like these.'

'Who told you they are honest?'

'Nobody has to tell me. I read. And because I am a journalist, I also write.'

'But look what it will do to our village. Finished. Who are we leaving it to? Who?'

'Who knows? I am sorry, but I have my life to live and I want it to be good.'

'Are we being selfish?' Dunstan asked.

'Perhaps we are,' said Robin and left it at that.

Good things were happening too. Marriages. They demolished the barriers between the three communities of Portuguese Christians: the East Indians, Goans and Mangaloreans. Patrades and xacuti were prepared in the same houses as tamriale and mutton kuddi. You heard Konkani mayayoes being sung at umbrachea paanis. It began to look like subsequent generations would not know if they were East Indian, Goan or Mangalorean. The now seniors, while they rejoiced at what was happening, expressed a fading hope that the different cultures would survive at least in the form of some fusion of language, cuisine, music and the quaint customs of the three communities. Some of it did. The cuisine, music and some customs were consciously preserved by at least a few, but already Konkani and East Indian Marathi were lost to the latest generation of Kevni-Amboliites. English and Hindi had taken over.

'Today it is happening to Kevni and Amboli,' said our local prophet, Stanny Rebello. 'Tomorrow it will happen to Mumbai. Wait and see. It will take a little time. Maybe forty-fifty-sixty years max. The children of tomorrow's Mumbai will not know whether they are Maharashtrian, Punjabi or Malayalee, nor will they care. Amor vincit omnia. Inter-marriage and education will do it. And then, my friends, I would like to see who will stand up and say Mumbai amchi.'

Stanny had seen it in his own family. His daughter, Shirley, was now daughter-in-law to the one-time staunch East Indian Fonsecas. The credit, he had to acknowledge had to go to Hazel, Shirley's sister-in-law, who in those early days of stubborn animosities took the ultimate step of leaving home and getting married to Cliffy. Or perhaps one had to hand it to Rahul, the grandson, whose birth changed everything—the Fonsecas had taken the predictable step of inviting their daughter home after delivery, unable to resist the tug of grandparenting. By that time, the Fonseca resistance to the marriage of Shirley and Dominic had become limp. It was a rollicking East Indian wedding, complete with umbrachea paani and all the horseplay that went with it.

Shirley lived with the Fonsecas until Dominic got his visa for Sharjah. Two decades and two children later, the Fonseca household, like the rest of the village, had become a soup bowl of East Indian, Mangalorean and Goan cultures.

Other barriers were crumbling. Between the haves and the have-nots; between those who had property and those who didn't; between those who had property and no cash and who had cash but no property. And those who had neither cash nor property but had that something else that changed their lives forever—education and a little vision.

With each holiday homecoming, Kitty and her friends noticed the change. Erstwhile chawl families walked with that glow of a big bank balance on their faces alongside sons and daughters with university degrees, most of them reeking of the fiscal perfumes of the new Arabia. Many of them had invested in that emerging fiduciary instrument—real estate. Some of them owned more than one apartment in the suburbs, yet continued to live in their chawls, anticipating that other windfall—redevelopment of their chawls by builders, where they could be entitled to 30 per cent more space in a modern apartment complex.

On the other hand, landlords of yesterday exchanged their valuable fixed assets for the unfixed worth of currency that failed to keep pace with the cost of living and their expectations. This sent them down a slide of lowering standards and, worse, perceived social status. It was not surprising to see many one-time 'aristocratic' families bleary-eyed as they stood still in the slough of sinking finances and lifestyle. A case in point was the third generation of Blaise Misquitta's family. The older two granddaughters, given in marriage to two young men from similar, 'decent' families, found themselves, not too long after their marriage, floundering in a situation close to penury while their husbands sat at home doing nothing, having frittered away cash and property.

Some of them fortunately found spouses for their children from among established wealthy families in the city and with young people—East Indian, Mangalorean, Goan—with degrees from foreign universities—who were now employed abroad. They took up residences further south of the city or emigrated to what they believed to be more a comfortable lifestyle.

Kitty's mind swung away from these thoughts back to the funeral. The priest had begun a racy recitation of Psalm 130, the De Profundis. 'From the depths, I have cried out to you, O Lord; Lord, hear my voice. Let your ears be attentive to the voice of my supplication…'

Kitty glanced at the time on her mobile phone. Austin was late. He had hoped to be in time for the funeral. They would soon be covering the coffin and the grave. She looked at the face in the casket. Did he too seem as if he was waiting for someone or something, Kitty wondered.

If you, Lord, were to mark iniquities,
who, O Lord, shall stand?
For with you is forgiveness …

She felt a tap on her shoulder. It was Austin, finally.

With him was Posco in a black tie. Austin had gone to pick him up at the airport so he could be in time to see his beloved guardian, the person who had found him in this very cemetery a little over a quarter of a century ago, had fed him and with the persuasion of his mumbling incoherence, got the principal of St. Blaise's School to make sure that Posco got a high-school education. All through school, Posco spent his free time at Ignatius' garage where he listened like a trained counsellor to the woes and joys of motorcars as articulated by their spark plugs, crank shafts and pistons. Ignatius let him work in his garage as the boy grew, marvelling at his way with machines. He seemed to need no training. It was as if he had been born with the drawing of the car's innards in his brain. After the SSC, it was Ignatius who sponsored Posco for a diploma course at the Agnel Technical Institute. Posco was grateful for all that.

At the grave, head bowed, he shed unashamed tears as he watched the serene face of his guardian.

The Sultan's Man

ON HIS SECOND DAY IN MUSCAT, POSCO FOUND HIMSELF in a hospital with serious injuries. It proved to be a life-changing event for him.

It was Mario from Amboli who had arranged a visa and a job for him as a helper in the PDO garage, where he would have to help with the maintenance of the company's fleet of vehicles. Posco was reluctant to take up the job because the man we know as Hanging Gardens, his guardian, was not keeping too well. The St. Vincent de Paul Society had arranged to have his hernia and hydrocele attended to. The surgery was done and he was back on his feet. Of late, however, he had slowed down. Age was catching up even with him. Carmine, the mother, had died a year ago, which meant that there would be nobody to look after the ageing man. Posco was advised by the St. Vincent de Paul Society to have him admitted into the senior citizens' home at Chakala, Andheri. He did this, promising to send money every month so Hanging Gardens would lack for nothing.

The day after his arrival in Muscat he had gone out to buy a few essentials when a Ferrari, which had obviously lost control, climbed the pavement and sped towards him. Posco did a quick sidestep but not quick enough to dodge the metal beast, which hit him and crashed against a pole.

Help arrived within minutes, not for Posco but for the Ferrari. Sirens wailed and cars with flashing lights screeched to a halt at the scene of the accident. The men who materialized almost from thin air had uniforms and badges identifying them as palace personnel. They extricated the driver (who happened to be the Sultan's aide) from behind the wheel. He was not hurt but was in a state of shock. The beautiful metal beast, now a little misshapen, was pushed and half-carried from the pavement onto the street. Men and tools went to work under the bonnet. The Ferrari, like all prima donnas, however was proving difficult. It wouldn't start. After many looks under the bonnet and vain attempts with the ignition, the men stood round the car looking helpless.

At that moment, the palace officials and mechanics saw a broken, bleeding body crawl towards the car, leaving a snaky trail of blood behind it. They knew it must be the accident victim. They watched as if paralyzed as the body painfully raised itself up to the level of the bonnet. Its hands reached inside and seemed to make some adjustments, like a conjurer doing some undercover sleight of hand. His spectators at that moment thought they heard soft strains of *Ave. Ave. Ave Maria* coming from the innards of the car. Weakly, the body's bloody face looked up and signalled to the men standing around the car to start it. The Ferrari roared to life.

Posco was driven to the hospital in the same car. He stayed there for over a week, being treated in a luxurious air-conditioned room of the best hospital in Muscat, with doctors and nurses ministering to him around the clock. He heard the hospital staff refer to him in hushed tones of awe as 'the Sultan's Man'.

On his discharge, he was driven in a huge sedan directly to the Sultan's palace. His mind was in a spin as he was brought into the presence of the Sultan, who told him that he no longer worked for the PDO and that from that day onwards he would be working in the Sultan's garage, looking after the large fleet of the palace's vehicles.

From then on it was a charmed life that broke through all barriers of probability, and which inspired incredulity at the pace and steepness of his climb to favour and wealth. Within a few months of working in the garage, the chief engineer was heard to say, 'This is no mechanic, he is a magician,' and it was not uncommon to hear strains of the *Ave* coming from all the other engineers and mechanics in the belief that it was some magical mantra that made engines obey their tools. It was not long before he was sent to the workshops and shop floors of the world's best car manufacturers to see how they worked, the last one of these being Rolls-Royce of England.

With every visit to India he tried to make the life of his guardian easier. He was able to buy a two-bedroom apartment. He brought Hanging Gardens home from the seniors' home and spent time with him, amusing him with pictures of Muscat and the Sultan's palace and garage. He told him that he could take him to Muscat, where he could live comfortably, but he was met with 'Anton happy in home. Posco happy in palace. Good. Let be.'

Posco found himself quietly giving large sums of money every month to the Misquitta daughters who had fallen on hard times. He had not forgotten the days when he sat in a corner of the Misquitta kitchen, partaking of meals from the Misquitta table with Carmine.

The fact is, just twenty years from the time he met his guardian at his mother's gravesite, Posco had become an incredibly rich man with apartments in Four Bungalows, Yaari Road and Kevni, the former two bought for the purpose of investment.

Kitty glanced sideways at Posco. He looked dignified even in his grief. His wealth showed on his face, not in any supercilious look of arrogance that one finds among the new rich, but in a look of refinement that spoke of a quiet acceptance of good fortune.

The Vote Banks

Stanny Rebello's prophecy sat like a cloud over that ribbon of a pathway dividing the two villages. On the sunrise side of it, the Salsette Catholic Cooperative Housing Society had its dream fulfilled in the shape of apartment houses, which the owners either sold or gave out on rent to anyone willing to pay the price. The new wave of migrants to this Kevni-Amboli annexe included Goans and Mangaloreans (many more of the latter) who were able to trade their poky little pugri-loaded homes in the city for these relatively more comfortable suburban apartments. St. Blaise's parish was threatening to be more 'Manggy' than East Indian.

It was on the sunset side of the ribbon that the prophecy was visibly fulfilled ('this place will never be the same,' Stanny had said) in that the Shiva temple and its political cousin, the Shiv Sena shakha, by its side gave rise to a cultural parallelism that did not find comfortable meeting points among the people. The earlier differences between the Goans, East Indians and Mangaloreans were slowly smoothed out via parish activity and, more recently, by marriage. This west side of the ribbon was different. And loud. Gaining decibels and muscle because of its alliance with a political party that was on the ascendance. Soon their numbers swelled and spilled on to the other side of the ribbon as well, with tenements popping up wherever there were blank spaces. The vote bank of the party was growing in size and influence. Between daylong chants and the clang of temple bells, the bright saffron flags and huge posters of the Sena's roaring tiger, the traditional manifestations of Amboli's character began to fade under this politico-religious crescendo. It was as if it were willingly surrendering to a stronger, more strident force. It was a smooth and easy takeover, however, with no trace of animosity or aggression between the sides. It was like an older, quieter voice allowing the younger, louder one to dominate the party conversation. There were even attempts at integration.

At a parish youth meeting, Stanny Rebello's son, Norbert, had suggested that the youth group and the Church itself reach out to the temple (not the Sena; politics, he said, should be kept out of this) in an attempt to integrate with this group.

'This is an opportunity for us to show other parishes the way forward,' he said when he was invited to speak on the role of the young. The youth group, under his leadership, had already been involved in ecumenical meetings with other Christians in the YWCA. He was also taking an active part in the work done in the slums on the other side of the highway, Majaswadi, a place they called Squatters' Colony. Sundays he would walk the distance from Amboli to Majaswadi and sit in the huts of the squatters there, drinking chai with them and discussing ways of shaking up the authorities for basic amenities like running water and sanitation. Father Lazarus, who went with them, had warned him to be careful, lest he run foul of the authorities who could set the police on him with all kinds of false allegations, but the young man seemed intent on what he was doing.

With cautious support from their spiritual director he organized a couple of bhajan sessions in the school hall in which a few temple singers joined the youth choir. The latter sang some of the raga-based Christian bhajans composed by Father Gyan Prakash. They were met with much curious interest at first on both sides, but after a couple of sessions, he noticed that the felt rewards were dwindling.

'I am not sure these people are interested,' he told his father. 'I see an artificial and strained camaraderie which will take us nowhere.'

'I think you are right,' Stanny said. 'There's no point continuing with it. At least you made an attempt,' he said by way of consolation.

Two months later, Norbert dropped a minor bombshell.

'Hey folks,' he told the family in a tone that was almost jocular. 'I am joining the priesthood. The Jesuits.'

After a short silence, his father said. 'I could see it coming.'

In his last year of graduation, Norbert had moved to St. Xavier's College in the city. His interaction with the Jesuits there made him all the more convinced that working with the marginalized and with religious groups other than Roman Catholic was a challenge he personally wanted to take up. He got interested in Liberation Theology and the ideas of Gustav Gutierez, Jon Sobrino and Gerard Ludwig Muller. He spent time with other students who felt similarly challenged. But there was always a feeling that the work he was doing then did not even touch the fringes of the results he had hoped for. He made a long trip with a couple of priests to Talasari in Palghar district and to Roha in Raigad. He came home from these trips looking gaunt and with his beard grown long. That's when he announced to his parents his decision to become a priest.

'Is it because of Kitty?' his mother asked. 'You know that many other girls are interested in you, putta.'

He laughed. 'You should have told me that before, Mother,' he said. 'I would have started chasing them myself, Now it is too late.'

'I am not unhappy,' Stanny said. 'He and I can have our fights regarding dogma, the clergy and ecclesiastical misdemeanour.'

'Trouble is,' said Norbert, 'I will find myself on your side most of the time.'

He told his parents that they had six months to prepare for the separation.

Norbert gave up his attempts to bring the culturally disparate groups in Amboli together. He knew that there were political ballasts involved here. Already there were other warring parties that were threatening the peace of the village. The Congress and the Communist Party had their irons in the fire. The Shiv Sena's splinter, the Maharashtra Navnirman Sena—the MNS—had their vote bank in the midst of another shanty cluster at the other end of Amboli, showing signs of more aggression than the one east of the ribbon. In a way, it provided a foil to their cousin the Shiv Sena, one that helped to bring about some equilibrium to a situation that at one time threatened to become troublesome. Between the various vote banks, Norbert came to the conclusion, with his father, that they had better let things be the way they were. Time would decide the fate and future shape of Amboli.

Patsy

THE FUNERAL PRAYERS HAD ENDED AND THE PRIEST sprinkled holy water over the body and passed the sprinkler around. The small group waited for a few minutes while the first clumps of earth covered the grave. They then began walking out of the cemetery.

Kitty turned back and began surveying the other graves. She read the names on the newer ones—the wooden crosses, the new niches and the marble slabs in the church porch. The Misquittas, Gomeses, D'mellos, the Pintos, Saldanhas and D'souzas; East Indians, Goans, Mangaloreans; acquaintances, friends, friends' parents; a whole generation of parishioners that together shaped the character of the villages. She stood for some minutes over the grave of Patsy and Freddy. She had missed their funerals but had heard all about them, the widespread grief at their passing, of how all of Amboli's youth clamoured to handle Patsy's casket as their legitimate right for at least two minutes each as the procession walked slowly to the church. All of Doris Terrace (that old stately landmark) had gone, the older generation to their graves, the younger to other climes. That little acre of music was gone. Kitty thought Doris Terrace could well be a metaphor for the rest of the village. The globe and the cemetery. Amboli's diaspora of the living and the dead.

The soul of Kevni and Amboli had trickled out with every funeral and immigration and all but made complete with the advent of political factions that sought to build their own vote banks, first within the crevices of a more or less homogeneous society and then broadening out along the periphery of the old villages to change for ever the face and soul of old Tristao Dias Ribeiro's jurisdiction.

The village and its original character was dying and making room for the infiltration of the city of Mumbai. To Kitty, it now looked like a place without character; a hodgepodge of cultures; an untidy bhel-puri; a messy salad bowl. But as she began to think of it with her journalistic sensitivities, she saw that the village was evolving the way it should. It was like all the old villages—Bandra, Santa Cruz, Kalina, Chakala—being absorbed in that big cultural soup bowl—Mumbai.

This was right and proper.

Going Home

As they were finally getting ready to leave the gravesite, Kitty saw a family enter the porch and move quickly to the cemetery. Something in the man's face told her that she had seen him before. He had come with a lady who was obviously his wife and their son who must have been around twelve years old. The lady was foreign looking, most likely British. Kitty stopped and made as if to follow them into the graveyard.

Austin held her hand and asked her, 'Where are you going?'

'I think I have seen him before,' she said.

They stopped and stood where they were. It was evening and the sun was beginning to set. In the fading light and the relative silence of that evening came a deep bass voice singing that piece from Dvorak's *New World Symphony*, 'Going home'.

Peter Miranda had finally come to see his half-brother. A few minutes too late.

Glossary/Translations

Page 1: ***baida***: Mumbai Hindi slang for 'egg'. Said to be a corruption of B.E.D.A., the Bombay Egg Dealers Association

Page 7: ***naka*** (Hindi/Marathi): junction

ghoda gaadi (Hindi/Marathi): horse carriage

Page 8: ***police chowki*** (Hindi/Marathi): police post. The word 'chowk' means a four-road crossing. Since the police posts were generally at these crossings, they were called chowkis.

havildar (Hindi/Marathi): police constable

Page 9: ***aai-chi-kit-kit***: literally 'mother's annoying nagging'. Expresses annoyance. 'Damn!'

handa (Marathi): vessel.

Page 16: ***bhel-puri*** (Hindi): a snack; a mixture of crisp roasted and fried nibbles, eaten with a deep-fried crackers

chintoo-pintoo (Hindi): slang for 'puny'. The rhyming double word is a frequently used form of colloquial emphasis in Hindi and Marathi.

Page 17: ***bibi*** (Managlorean Konkani): slang for 'penis'

Page 19: **kunbi** (Marathi): the farmer community among East Indians

koli (Marathi): the fishing community among East Indians

Page 20: **pakad thyala** (East Indian Marathi): Catch him

Page 29: **Somya kakut kor** (Konkani): Lord have mercy

Page 30: **kudd** (Konkani): room. In this case, the kudd refers to an institution set up by Goans in Bombay to provide dormitory facilities for Goan bachelors

Page 36: **mara mereko** (Mumbai Hindi); **marla mala** (Marathi): (He) hit me

sorry bolaila ala (Marathi): came to say sorry

sorry munn, re (Konkani): say 'sorry'

borem bashen munn, re (Konkani): say it nicely.

Page 36: **tula** (East Indian Marathi): for you

Page 56: **gauthan** (Marathi): village boundary

Page 57: **nauvari sari** (Marathi): the traditional nine-yard sari

langoti (Marathi): triangular cloth used as loincloth/jock by men

Page 58: **gumat** (Marathi): a local drum made out of an earthen pot and stretched skin—usually the skin of the monitor lizard

Page 69: **patrade** (Konkani): a particularly Mangalorean snack made from the leaves of a water lily

Page 79: **chattambade** (Konkani): snack made from chickpea paste

Page 85: **bhandari** (Marathi): the toddy-tapper community

Page 86: **hand breads**: hand-flattened bread made from boiled rice flour dough

kuddi, lonwas: East Indian curries; the first made with roasted coconut and the latter with coconut milk

hajampatti (Hindi): literally 'shaving'. Colloquial for wasting time

Page 87: **nowra-baiko** (Marathi): husband and wife

Page 107: **tabela** (Hindi): cattle shed

Page 111: **'Hey bachcha. Hutto. Jao.'** (Hindi): Hey, kiddo. Move on. Go.

Page 127: **chedua** (Konkani): my girl

Page 128: **lafda** (Hindi): problem; messy affair

log ktte kitte muntat (Konkani): people say all kinds of things, blabber

Page 130: **kitte muntai go, chedua!** (Konkani): what are you saying, my girl?

Page 135: **kaabaar** (Konkani): finished

Page 140: **maana** (Konkani): literally older sister. Colloquial: plane Jane

Page 163: **padvigaar** (Konkani): parish priest

Page 184: **Chandamama** (Marathi): the moon. Literally, 'Uncle Moon'

Page 188: **bagha** (Marathi): look

Page 207: **paithyoos** (East Indian Marathi): old men

Page 209: **xacuti** *pronounced 'shakuti'* (Goan Konkani): Goan coconut-based curry

mayayoes: chorus to a number of Konkani folk songs

umbrachea paani (Marathi): ceremonial bathing of the bride and groom. The bride or groom is taken with much fanfare to the village well, where water is collected to give him/her a bath.

Acknowledgements

One way or the other, I would have written this novel. The story just typed itself out on my laptop from the tangled threads in my head.

But once written, the thing would lie there as so many used up kilobytes, picked up and read only by its author. Fortunately there was Ingrid, my wife, who from time to time peers over my shoulder to see what's happening on my screen, much in the manner of checking if the rice pot has come to a boil. When Ingrid sees something she likes very much, she cries. She cried. That encouraged me. I am grateful for that tearful encouragement…

On Ingrid's goading, I emailed the file to Robin, my brother, and Lorna, my sister, who gave me the nod of approval. I am grateful. Robin's wife, Teresa, even awarded me her personal Booker Prize. I am grateful.

Rohan, my son, and his colleague, Pavitra, were the ones who assured me they would find a publisher. That was encouraging and I am grateful. But then, it was Kanishka

Gupta of Writers' Side who gave me the big Yes, and waved the thing in front of the Speaking Tiger. Thank you Kanishka.

It is to Ravi Singh and his team I owe my biggest thank you. Aruna Ghose has had to spend hours going through the manuscript and getting it fit for a Speaking Tiger publication. I am grateful.

A writer is deeply grateful to every single person who reads his book. I dreamed I wrote out a million thank yous. One of them is to you, with this book in your hand.

I am grateful.

IA